Copyright © 2019 Brianna Skylark

All rights reserved.

ISBN-13: 9781088708538

This is a work of fiction. Names, characters, places, and incidents either are the product of the author's imagination or are used fictitiously. Any resemblance to actual persons, living or dead, events, or locales is entirely coincidental.

Copyright © 2019 by Brianna Skylark.

All rights reserved. No part of this publication may be reproduced, distributed, or transmitted in any form or by any means, including photocopying, recording, or other electronic or mechanical methods, including information storage and retrieval systems, without the prior written permission of the author, except in the case of brief quotations embodied in critical reviews and certain other noncommercial uses permitted by copyright law.

First edition August 2019.

www.briannaskylark.com

SHARING ROSE

BRIANNA SKYLARK

Rose has always wanted them, but she could never have them. Not both of them... at the same time. It wouldn't be right... it would be naughty.

Jacob and Alex have known Rose for ten years, and they've loved her since the day they all met, but three years ago she ran away. Now she's back and they're not letting her go... even if it means having to share.

Three friends; two men and one delicate Rose.

Jacob and Alex are inseparable, and that's exactly how Rose wants them. But after seven years being seen as nothing more than a friend, Rose couldn't take it anymore and ran away.

When a camping trip in the Alps brings them back together again three years later, Rose begins to wonder if her fantasy of the pair having their way with her could come true after all.

Or could the reunion reignite old rivalries, and drive them all apart for good? If it's worth having... is it worth sharing?

A Rose between two thorns... beneath a blanket of stars.

CHAPTER ONE

As the wheels of the aircraft touched down on the asphalt at Geneva Airport, Rose felt a wave of excitement wash over her. The journey had been smooth and on time, and as the plane had descended through the thin layer of golden cloud, the views across the crescent shape of Lake Geneva had been breathtaking.

Rose had watched with wide eyes as the plane had banked across the huge stretch of water which split the border between Switzerland and France, the sun reflecting off the surface like a swarm of golden fireflies. As the aircraft had continued to circle, the imposing sight of Mont Blanc had come into view to the south, its snow topped peaks and glacial northern slope appeared at once to be both glorious and intimidating.

Now as the plane slowed down, swerving gently from side to side as the brakes brought it to a stop, she felt elated and more than a little giddy. There were so many reasons for her to be excited.

For one, she was here for three nights of hiking in the Swiss Alps, which was, as far as Rose was concerned, the most beautiful place on earth. As a Geography graduate, she was in heaven.

Secondly, she was going to be wild camping which was her favourite type of camping experience, bringing her closer to nature, and as a budding conservationist, this was immensely important to her.

Finally though, and the real reason she was feeling both exhilarated and nauseous with anticipation, was that she would be doing this with her two oldest and closest friends, Alex and Jacob.

Rose had known *the boys* for ten years, since the very first days of secondary school. Back then, they had been summarily thrown together from different schools across the county, and whilst many of their classmates had arrived in pairs or more from the various feeder schools, Alex, Jacob and Rose were alone.

It didn't take the three of them long to find this small piece of common ground and by the end of the first day, Rose had lost all of the feelings of trepidation, intimidation and loneliness that had consumed her for much of the last few days of that long, hot summer.

Her family had moved down to the south of England from Edinburgh after her father's job had forced him to relocate. He had managed to hold off moving the whole family until she had finished primary school, but over the course of that summer, Rose had said goodbye to her friends, (promising to stay in touch with a select few) spent quality time with her extended family, and cleared out a lot of old belongings, including a few beloved toys. It had been a painful time for her, and for her parents, but starting at a new school in a new part of the country, was exciting and she had been looking forward to it, even if she was a little nervous.

By the end of their first week at school, they were inseparable and although at times it had been complicated and confusing, they had navigated the next seven years together as close friends until they had parted ways for University. Although perhaps *parted ways* wasn't entirely accurate.

Whilst Alex and Jacob had opted to stay in the area, applying for courses at their local University, she had left to live and study amongst the rugged mountains of Snowdonia in the north of Wales.

Now, three years later, she was taxiing across the runway of Geneva International Airport, less than half an hour away from seeing them again.

She had flown in from Manchester on an early morning flight having spent the night in an airport hotel reminiscing about their adventures together and stalking the pair of them on social media, obsessing over whether some of the girls in the various photos they had posted over the last year were girlfriends or ex-girlfriends or potential future girlfriends and then realising she was acting unnecessarily possessive about two boys (now men, she had to keep reminding herself, but they would always be the boys in her mind) whom she no longer really knew.

The plane came to a gentle stop at the gate and as soon as the seatbelt sign flickered off, she was up like a shot, popping open the overhead baggage and sliding out her cabin bag sized rucksack. She was near the rear of the plane, two rows forward from the toilets, which was always a bit of gamble but this time it paid off as the rear cabin door was unsealed and she was able to make a quick exit, stepping out into the bright sunshine and the crisp morning air.

The noise of the airport was a little disorienting but she made her way down the stairs and stayed between the painted pedestrian lines as she walked into the terminal. Inside she began to follow the arrows to the arrivals area, her excitement building. As she got closer she started to wonder if the boys would be waiting for her behind the exit barrier, holding up an embarrassing placard and grinning like a pair of morons.

She giggled to herself, drawing a brief disinterested glance from a fellow passenger as they stepped onto the travelator beside one another.

She had butterflies in her stomach.

She hadn't felt the sensation since she'd lost her virginity in the back of her first boyfriend's car. The intrusive memory burst into her mind, and for a moment she pictured her fumbling, somewhat embarrassing first time, as Stanley, the floppy haired wannabe rockstar awkwardly humped her for a few minutes on the back seat, as she tried to ignore the cramp building in her leg. The act itself had been satisfactory, if a little painful, but the anticipation had been intense and exhilarating.

She loved the feeling as it coursed through her body again, like a flood of adrenaline. It was making her feel more than a little aroused and she had to get control of herself.

She remembered how much Alex and Jacob had hated Stanley and had barely spoken to her whilst she dated him. She hadn't dared to tell them that she'd slept with him, but it didn't take long for them to find out after Stan the Man had bragged to all their friends about banging *Primroses's* bush.

Alex had come to college the following day with a bloodied fist, claiming he'd been in a fight and Jacob had been sullen and withdrawn for a week.

The whole episode had confused and upset Rose, but their relationship had recovered quickly, much to Rose's frustration, and before long they were all acting as if nothing had happened. Except for Stanley (who she'd dumped), who had still been proudly proclaiming his conquest to anyone who would listen, which turned out to be an awful lot of people. He probably still was.

She hadn't slept with Stanley because she loved him, or because she even liked him really. He was good looking in a traditional sort of way and he was a talented musician, arrogant and aggressively sure of himself, but that wasn't the reason she'd done it.

The real reason was that she was in love with both Jacob and Alex, and no matter how much she had tried to make this apparent to them, they had stubbornly failed to do anything about it.

At seventeen she was fickle, one week she would love Alex, the next Jacob, but it was always them and always had been. Eventually though, it became apparent to her that they either weren't interested, or had no intention of declaring their love for her, at least she thought so anyway. To them she seemed to be nothing more than their bratty little sister. But to her, they were her boys.

She had slept with Stanley to make them angry. And it had worked, and in some strange way that had made Rose happy. But then within a few short days, everything had gone back to normal and it had frustrated and upset her so much that when it came time to decide where to go to University she had chosen one hundreds of miles away from either of them.

She had done so to get away, because to have stayed would have broken her heart.

Since then she'd had a string of boyfriends, one night stands, and relationships, but there was one thing that was consistently wrong with each one.

They were not Jacob, nor were they Alex.

More than once she had lain awake at night and thought about them as she'd touched herself. Or laid back and pretended that the man fucking her was either one of her men. Sometimes both.

Often both.

Over time however, she had begun to heal, and it was going so well.

Until last week.

*

The email from the boys had come as a surprise.

When she'd left for University, they had all parted in good faith and Rose had promised them both that she would call, text and write to them all the time and that they could both visit whenever they wanted, but she hadn't intended to keep her word.

She had hated lying to them, but she'd had to do it. If she kept on thinking that one day, they would realise that she loved them and they in turn, would then love her back, then she would lose her mind.

So to start with she had kept up the pretence. If she had cut them out, they would've thought something was wrong and charged up to Wales like a couple of bulls, ready to smash up the china shop. So for the first few weeks, she had kept to her promise.

Then as time went on, it became easier. The messages became shorter, and fewer and farther between.

She dropped the names of a few boys she'd met, and made it seem like she was happy.

In truth, she was happy. Although she missed them both dearly. But it was working, little by little.

She dated, she kissed, she made love, and slowly, she forgot, and after the first year, Alex and Jacob had started to seem like a schoolgirl fantasy.

But it was a fantasy, and it was one she often came back to. So whilst she no longer saw them every day, she thought of them often.

Often improperly.

When the email came she was walking back to her flat share from her part time job working at an outdoor hiking shop in the main high street. The money wasn't great, but she was managing to pay rent and save a little whilst she applied for jobs working in conservation and habitat management. She'd had an interview a few days before, which she felt had gone well and she was expecting an email back from the organisation any day now, so hitting the refresh button on her inbox was becoming a relentless habit.

It was raining and her umbrella was struggling in the gusts of wind that were blowing down the street towards her. She had flipped her phone out of her pocket again and hit refresh and was about to slip it back inside the waterproof lining when she saw something unusual.

Jacob's name had appeared.

She slowed to a halt as she saw it and as she did the wind turned her umbrella inside out.

She read the name again, wondering if it was just a spam message from a similar name, or maybe his account had been hacked and the email would be inviting her to *click here to read the rest of my message*.

She hadn't heard from either of them in more than two and half years.

She tapped on the email.

Hi Rose,

How are you? We miss you! Alex and I were wondering if you're doing anything next week? We know it's short notice, but we're flying out to Switzerland for a few days hiking in the Alps and we'd love to have you come and join us. It's been a long time, and we figured that now we've all finished Uni, why don't we get together for one more adventure before we all head out into the world of work. Jacob and I are actually going travelling together for a whole year soon so it would be really great if we could see you before we head off on our round the world adventure. Don't worry if you can't, we understand (but would be gutted!), but do let us know if you can make it. We're flying out on the 8th.

Love Jacob and Alex

XxX

She stood still, the rain filling up her upturned umbrella. Half way through reading the email for a second time the umbrella tipped over, but Rose barely registered it.

A few days hiking in the Alps? She loved the Alps. She suddenly felt sick.

She couldn't possibly say yes, it would destroy all the progress she had made over the last three years. She hadn't even thought about them in a long time.

Well that wasn't strictly true.

She hadn't thought about them socially, in a long time, but they were never far from her thoughts on a lonely night.

What harm could a few days do though, really?

No.

She would delete the email, or mark it as spam and pretend she never saw it.

She slipped her phone back into her jacket, righted her umbrella and headed back in the direction of her flat.

When she got there, after fumbling the key in the lock as the rain continued to pour down, she opened the door to the sound of her flatmate, Amber, shagging her new boyfriend Matt.

The sound was slightly muffled, and initially, as Rose hung up her wet coat and spread out her umbrella to dry, she thought they were both upstairs.

So when she opened the kitchen door to find Amber bent

over the work surface, knickers around her ankles as Matt fucked her from behind, it came as a bit of a shock.

'Oh shit, I'm sorry,' said Rose, and slammed the door closed, turning around and heading upstairs to her own room.

As she got part way up the stairs she heard Amber calling after.

'Rose?'

She kept on going and reached the landing before Amber (who was still pulling up her knickers) appeared at the bottom of the stairs.

'Rose, I'm so sorry.'

'It's fine,' she said. 'Carry on,' before closing her bedroom door.

She sat down on her bed, utterly mortified, trying to shake the image of Matt thrusting into her friend. Then she heard them talking quietly.

'Is she okay?' said Matt.

'I don't know, she just said to carry on,' said Amber.

Matt laughed. 'Bit late,' he said.

'Oh gross,' said Amber. 'Clear it up.'

'Why don't you see if she wants to join us?'

'Don't be a dick, Matt.'

'She's hot, I'd love a go.'

'Fuck off, put your fucking trousers back on and clean the fucking floor. You're such a dick sometimes.'

'You love it.'

Rose turned on the radio, she'd heard enough.

She lay back on her single bed, the wind whistling in through the small gap in the double hung window, and looked up at the gradually spreading damp patch on the ceiling and made up her mind.

She picked up her phone, found Jacob's email and began to reply.

* * *
*

Rose was even more breathtaking than Jacob had remembered.

He had seen her straight away, as soon as she had stepped through the arrivals gate, and for a brief second he was back at school, eagerly waiting for her to walk through the door of their classroom in the morning.

Jacob had spent the majority of his teenage years, desperately and hopelessly in love with Rose. She had been kind, sweet, funny, and boundlessly enthusiastic. He still vividly remembered the first time he ever saw her, all those years ago on the very first day of school.

As the new starters had gathered together after filing in through the school gates, they had been assembled in the sports hall to be introduced to their new headmistress before their induction sessions. Jacob didn't know anyone, having moved to the area with his family over the summer before and at that point, surrounded by hundreds of other children who were laughing and joking together as they'd all filed in, he had started to become tearful.

Several teachers had welcomed them into the hall and spread them out in a large horseshoe around the central stage where a podium and microphone had been erected for the head. As the voices of all the children became hushed, Jacob who had been lined up on the front row, had looked down in shame to hide his tear filled eyes, but as he'd done so he had caught sight of someone looking at him.

He'd looked up and met the gaze of a young, fearless and pretty little red haired girl looking straight at him and smiling. He had immediately begun to blush, and with the sleeve of his jumper, he'd quickly wiped his eyes in a vain attempt to hide his tears, but it was clear that this girl was looking at him and knew that he was crying. Jacob's lower lip had wobbled as he had waited for her to point and laugh, but to his surprise, she did neither. Instead she had winked and flashed him such a brilliant smile that he had immediately felt happier, and had smiled back.

Jacob knew right away that he wanted to be her friend.

As the headmistress had arrived and given her welcome speech, Jacob had repeatedly found himself drawn to looking over at his new friend, and whenever he did, she would glance back and smile and he would look away. Over the course of the brief assembly, it had become a game of sorts. Jacob would turn his head to look over at her, to see that she would be looking away, up at the ceiling or toward a teacher and then her head would snap back and her eyes would flash as he tried his best to look in another direction before her eyes met his.

By the end of the assembly, Jacob had found himself wishing that this girl might be in his class, so he would have an opportunity to talk to her. He was naturally shy, but this girl was so confident and full of energy that it had been practically infectious.

As the assembled students had departed the hall, Jacob had lost sight of his new friend and as he'd desperately searched for her he'd seen a boy, with dark olive skin, looking around a little forlorn as all the other children chatted and giggled with one another.

His confidence boosted by the fun he'd had during the assembly, he'd decided to approach this boy and introduce himself.

'Hi, I'm Jacob,' he'd said.

'Alex,' said the boy. 'What form are you?'

'Osborne.'

'Me too,' said Alex. 'Do you want to be friends?'

With Alex by his side, Jacob and he had found their form

room quickly and easily, and filed inside, to be greeted by their new tutor and much to Jacob's excitement, he saw that the red haired girl was there too. She was sat alone at one of the tables, smiling happily and kicking her legs back and forth.

Jacob had grabbed Alex's arm and tugged him in her direction and the two had gone over to introduce themselves to the girl who would become their friend, and although Jacob didn't quite understand it yet, he had already begun to fall in love with her.

Now here she was, ten years later. Grown up, mature, intelligent, driven and passionate, and as she caught sight of them both, Jacob immediately started to regret everything that had led up to this point.

'Rose,' he called out and waved the stupid placard he and Alex had made together the night before. It was drawn on the back of a menu, taken from the hotel they were staying at, situated just a few minutes drive from the airport.

Their creation was a badly drawn bunch of flowers in the shape of the word *Prim*, Rose's nickname from school. They'd put quite a lot of effort into it and thought it was incredibly funny at the time, but it now seemed somewhat childish and Jacob felt more than a little ashamed as Rose approached, smiling with a beguiling radiance.

They had arrived a day early to arrange car hire and organise everything, booking a hotel for a few nights to have somewhere they could leave their belongings, registering their route with the local authorities in case something happened, prepaying for long term parking at the entrance to the trail, and then finally relaxing in the evening for a few beers before Rose arrived.

Now she was walking towards them and Jacob was enchanted once again.

'Oh my goodness,' she said, holding her hands over her

eyes and face as she drew near. 'I have missed you both so much.'

She leaned in to hug them and the two of them embraced her, wrapping their large arms around her lithe figure and squeezing her tightly.

'It's so good to see you,' she said whispering. She turned her head to kiss Alex and then Jacob on the cheek and pulled back, wiping away an embarrassing tear and smiling. She laughed as she realised there was little point in trying to hide her emotions.

'You're late,' said Alex, still holding her by the waist.

'Oh sod off,' she said, pushing him away playfully. 'I told you I couldn't get here any earlier, besides I didn't want to intrude on the bromance.'

'You didn't miss much,' said Alex, putting his arm around Jacob's shoulder. 'We spent most of the night drawing this stupid placard and drinking Swiss beer in the hotel bar. But tonight,' he waved his hand up theatrically in a wide arc. 'We're all going to be sleeping under a blanket of stars.'

'I'm so excited,' she said. 'I did so much wild camping on Snowdon, but this is going to be something else.'

'You look incredible, Rose,' said Jacob. The three of them fell into a brief but awkward silence.

Rose flashed a coy smile at him. 'Thank you,' she said.

'I mean you look really well,' he said, quickly. 'Physically.'

Alex tried not to laugh, but found it too hard. 'Smooth, Jacob.'

'Don't,' said Rose, admonishing him. 'It's fine, thank you, Jacob. You guys don't look half bad yourselves, I'm guessing you found your way to a gym at last?'

'Four times a week,' said Alex. 'Even persuaded Jacob here to join.'

Rose was aware she was making an understatement, the pair of them looked chiseled. The last time she'd seen them, they were both tall and thin but now they had filled out into their bodies, and Alex's shirt rippled with muscle. His olive skin seemed to have darkened too. She wasn't sure if it was a tan or just age, but he looked incredible. Combined with his shaved head and dark, trimmed stubble, it was all a little too much. She was aware that several other women around the departure lounge were stealing glances in their direction.

Jacob looked handsome too, though he had a more understated appearance, not as bold as Alex's, but strong and powerful. His blonde hair seemed to have darkened and become more sandy since she'd last seen him and he'd styled it short, with shaven back and sides and a rough swoop, like he'd just rolled out of bed. Whilst he was clearly more confident than before, he still had a certain charming, British awkwardness that she loved.

'How was your flight?' said Jacob, eager to move on past his embarrassing outburst.

'Quiet,' said Rose. 'It was a nice change of pace actually, I spent most of the flight listening to an audiobook with my eyes closed.'

'What's your usual pace?'

'Breakneck these days, I'm applying for jobs in conservation but they're highly contested in my field. Something like sixty applicants to every position offered.'

'You're not in demand then? I find that hard to believe. Shall we get moving?' said Alex, picking up Rose's luggage.

'Oh, you don't need to take that,' she said.

But Alex waved his hand and smiled. 'It's not far to the car park.'

They walked side by side, Rose in the middle of the two men, eagerly chatting.

'So you guys are going travelling for a year? That's amazing. Where are you going to go?'

'We're planning to follow the old Silk Road. We're starting

off in France, then we're going to work our way east and finish off in Japan,' said Jacob, chiming in after feeling a little left out of the conversation so far.

'We're gonna book the most expensive room we can afford in the tallest skyscraper we can manage in Tokyo as our final treat,' interjected Alex, taking back control of the conversation again.

'Oh gosh, what an adventure. I'm so jealous. When do you leave?'

'Next month, twenty six days from now,' said Alex as he pressed the call button for the lift to the parking garage.

'I'd love to go travelling but I'm hoping I can do it as part of a new job. I had an interview for a position with an organisation that monitors wetland habitats two weeks ago and if I get it, I'd have the opportunity to travel all over the world.'

'Do you think you will?' said Alex.

The lift arrived and they all stepped in. Rose turned to face him, her back to Jacob.

'I think I might, I'm through to the next round of interviews, and the woman who would be my manager was really impressed with the work I did during my course. So I'm really hopeful.'

'Shit, Prim. You're like a rocket, shooting for the moon.' Alex whooshed his hand up into the air. 'Sounds like you're doing great,' he said laughing.

Jacob was starting to feel like an outsider now, a feeling he was starting to remember was common place when they were younger. The three of them seemed to be very quickly falling back into their old routines and for the second time since Rose had reappeared in their lives, he found himself feeling worried.

The lift door opened and they headed out into the garage. Alex leading the way to the car as the other two followed.

Rose on the other hand, was trying her very best not to skip.

*

CHAPTER TWO

It was a short drive from the airport to the hotel and Jacob and Alex had been considerate enough to allow time for Rose to shower, get changed and get ready for the three hour drive to the starting point of their first day of hiking in the Alps.

Rose had no idea what sort of adventure they had planned for them, but Alex had dropped a few hints as they'd discussed the trip over email, so she'd done her best to pack for a few eventualities.

But for now, Rose had an hour to unwind from her flight in the comfort of a private room as the men enjoyed a coffee downstairs whilst preparing for the lengthy drive ahead. She made herself a complimentary chamomile tea from the basket of assorted packets underneath the cheap little flatscreen television that was mounted on the wall. There was a strange game show playing where the contestants were bobbing for apples in some sort of unpleasant looking gloop. She turned down the volume and walked over to the window, breathing in the steam from her cup. Outside was a small park and in the distance the snow capped peaks of the Alps.

She sat down on the bed behind her and then lay down against the pillow. The covers had been badly made, thrown together by Alex or Jacob, she wasn't sure who. She breathed in deeply, her nose filling with scent of one of the men, her eyes closed.

Back when they were in school she would often borrow jumpers or hoodies from them, taking them home overnight and keeping them, sometimes for weeks on end and she would lay them beside her pillow and bury her face in the material if she was feeling lonely.

The clock on the side of the bed rolled over the hour and reminded her that she didn't have long.

She stripped down and left her clothes and underwear strewn across the twin beds, smiling to herself as though she was marking her territory and then tip-toed naked into the bathroom, turning the dial on the shower up high, and enjoying the steam as it permeated her nostrils and invigorated her skin.

Her thoughts quickly wandered back to Jacob's complimentary outburst at the airport. She knew he hadn't meant to be quite so forward, that had never been his style. Perhaps he had changed at University and become a little more confident and suave, but Rose wasn't some girl he'd met at freshers night. The way he'd said it, and the way he'd tried to cover it up had meant something, she was sure of it, but she wasn't sure what.

Or she was reading too much into it. She had wasted a lot of her time at school, reading too much into Alex or Jacob's behaviour.

She lathered up a small bar of travel soap in her hands and began to wash, letting the warm water cascade over her face and down her body.

Alex was acting different too, at least to how she remembered him. He was cocky and confident, and she'd liked it, a lot. Both of them had changed so much in three years, and she had too but the difference didn't feel quite so stark to her.

She realised that she was doing it again. What she had done to herself so many times throughout the last two years of school and all through her time in college; overthinking everything that the two boys did or said. It was like the last three years hadn't even happened, she had slipped straight back into obsessing over them, and she'd only been back alongside them for just over an hour.

She rubbed the soap gently into her stomach, letting the warm water wash away down her legs where it gathered in bubbles around her feet and between her toes, and then she looked up into the stream of water and let it flow over her face.

She couldn't help it though. The two of them were her boys. From the day they had met on the first day of school, she had sensed a connection between them all. Something beyond friendship, something powerful and raw and full of energy and love.

At the time she just wanted them to be friends forever. But as she'd grown up, she had started to think about them more and more. To start with she would have week long crushes on either one. Doodling their name for hours or dreaming of becoming Mrs Jacob or Mrs Alex, then, as she grew older, she began to fantasise about them.

She'd wanted them to take her, to make her theirs, to have their way with her and do whatever they wanted, whenever they wanted. To leave her breathless and satisfied yet desperate for more every day. But she knew it could never happen, that it was unconventional and outrageous. Filthy even.

Which of course, had just made her want it even more.

Her wet fingers brushed across her pussy as she recalled the fantasy that had brought her to orgasm so many times as she'd grown up. She closed her eyes as she quickened her touch, slipping her fingers up and down herself and leaning back against the wall of the shower.

It always started the same. The three of them in her dorm room at University, playing a game together on her little television set. Rose lying flat on her stomach, wearing just a t-shirt and her underwear, as the two of them sat either side of her, their interest divided between her almost bare bottom and the screen.

She pressed her fingers against her clit as she began to play it back again in her mind.

Her foot twitched as Alex's fingers tickled her, trying to distract her from beating his high score and she kicked him away as he persisted, trying his best to put her off.

'Get off, Alex,' she said.

'You're not going to beat me,' he said laughing and grabbing her foot. 'Grab the other one, Jacob. Hold her down.'

Jacob laughed and Rose reacted too late as he gripped hold of her right foot and held it tight. Laughing she tried desperately to keep playing as the two boys tickled the soles of her feet relentlessly, but it was no good, she was already losing and she watched in dismay, amongst fits of giggles, as her character died, not quite besting Alex's score.

'I can't believe you just did that,' she said, rolling over to admonish the pair of them and dropping the controller onto the carpet. 'You two owe me.'

'Oh yeah, and what do we owe you? Another ass kicking?' said Alex.

Rose turned back to look at them, squinting her eyes.

'One full body rub. Right now,' she said.

Alex laughed.

'A full body rub?' he nodded. 'Fine, deal. On your front, Prim.'

He knelt up on the bed, as Jacob sat back.

'From both of you,' said Rose, looking at Jacob and widening her eyes.

'You heard the girl, Jacob,' said Alex, grinning. 'She wants us both.'

'Hang on,' said Rose, as she stood up and put her hair back up into a pony tail, sliding a hair band off her wrist. She gestured for them both to move aside as she lay down on her front again along the length of her bed, stretching her arms out to the side.

In the shower, Rose quivered and pushed her fingers inside herself, biting her lip as she pictured the scene.

'Now you can start,' she said.

Jacob was on one side of the bed, and Alex was on the other, both standing still.

'Come on,' she said, and wiggled her bottom.

A moment later she felt Alex's hands in the middle of her back, and then Jacob's by her feet and she began to melt.

Little by little, the two of them caressed and squished and massaged her body, inch by inch from her toes to her thighs, and then back to her shoulders, and finally her neck and her head, Jacob running his fingers through her hair as her whole body tingled.

Then she realised that Alex wasn't touching her and as she looked back she could see that he was removing his trousers.

'What are you doing?' she said.

'Seemed like it might be easier this way,' came the reply, and then he was up on the bed and straddling her, sitting just below her bottom and pinning her down, his muscly and strong legs either side of her.

Then his hands were just above her waist, but this time

beneath her t-shirt. She bit her lip and settled her head down in the pillow and Alex's fingers inched their way up her spine against her skin.

Now she could hear that Jacob was doing the same, pulling down his trousers near to her head. She wanted to look, but she kept her eyes screwed shut.

A moment later she felt his hands sliding into either side of the arms of her t-shirt and caressing her back and shoulders, leaning over her, his bulge inches from her face.

Alex was leaning forward now, his hands all the way up the back of her shirt, so it was bunched up underneath her and pushing against her breasts and then she felt another sensation.

Alex's cock, pressing against her ass.

She breathed deeply as she felt it moving against her, her mouth going dry with excitement. Opening her eyes she found that Jacob's bulging boxers were barely hiding his cock and she had to resist reaching out to touch it. Instead she closed her eyes again, and then parted her legs ever so slightly.

Alex responded by sliding up her back again, pressing himself against her once more, but this time as his hands glided back down her body, he slid them onto her rump, pulling the edge of her underwear down a few inches and exposing just a little of her bottom.

She couldn't help but let out a whimper, then she bit her lip to stop herself moaning again.

'You two think you're going to fuck me or something?' she said, but it was barely a whisper.

A second later, she felt Jacob's cock pressing against her mouth, and she opened her lips and let him inside, his member gliding over her tongue.

As he slid deeper into her mouth, she felt Alex's fingers loop around the edge of her knickers and slide them down past her knees before he straddled her again, resting his cock between her cheeks and sliding it up and down.

Then suddenly, he was laying down against her back and his knees were pushing her legs apart, his cock sliding up against her soaking wet opening.

'You're ours now,' said Alex, whispering into her ear and then he slid into her.

The water was starting to go cold, but Rose didn't care. Her fingers were moving fast inside her now and the rest of the fantasy was running through her mind like a highlight reel.

She pictured Jacob kissing her lips as Alex kissed her neck and she moaned in pleasure. She writhed in time with Alex's imaginary thrusts into her from behind, and pretended her fingers were his cock in her pussy, as she slid them in and out herself, bringing herself quickly to orgasm as her legs began to shudder.

She climaxed as she imagined them both pumping inside her at the same time and then her legs gave way and she slipped down into a small heap as the water cascaded over her shaking body.

As she sat there on the floor, the warm torrent running down her face, she found she was suddenly feeling overcome with emotion.

She had spent so much of her life wanting them, and then she had run away and now she was back here with them again, laying down on their bed and smelling their pillows and showering in their bathroom and masturbating to the thought of them.

She started to sob.

To begin with it was quiet and reserved, but before long she was crying hard, the flood gates opening, her body wracked with emotion and regret and longing, but most of all with unrequited love.

* * *
*

Half an hour later, Rose emerged from the room, dressed and ready to go with her rucksack slung over her shoulder. She trotted down the stairs, feeling better after a good cry and bounced into the restaurant. She knew she was overcompensating, just like that first day of school. Inside she was a mess, but on the outside she was confident, exuberant and calm.

She smiled as the two men looked up and tried not to swoon as Alex winked at her as she approached.

A few minutes later they were outside with their three rucksacks stowed neatly in the rear of the small rental car, Rose's in the middle squished between the two men's larger bags. Jacob held the rear door open for Rose and she hopped in, grateful for the back seats to herself so she might stretch out a little after the cramped flight.

She watched as he then walked around to the passenger door and jumped in next to Alex, who started the engine as Jacob fastened his seatbelt. Alex's self-assurance had caused a stir in Rose, but Jacob's gentlemanly gestures and thoughtful behaviour were just as attractive.

She had to stop thinking like this, or she was going to end up in trouble, or worse still, an emotional wreck again, she thought to herself, as they pulled out of the small hotel car park and onto the slip road that led down and onto the autobahn.

The car vibrated as they crossed over the rumble strip into the outer lane and Rose had to adjust her posture to stop the sensation arousing her more so than she already was.

'How you doing back there?' said Alex as he pushed his foot down on the accelerator. She saw his eyes glancing between her and the road ahead as he drove.

'Excited,' said Rose.

'You've been to Switzerland before though, right?'

Rose smiled to herself as she realised that Alex must have snooped through her social media too. Had she noticed a little glance of concern from Jacob too? Worried that Alex might have given away too much?

'Yeah that's right. I flew over around two years ago, during my first year at Bangor. It was a field trip to study the Alpine ibex.'

'What's that?'

'It's a sort of horned mountain goat,' she said. 'They live high up on steep slopes in the Alps. We flew into Zurich and stayed near Pontresina? They actually come down into the village in spring but we came in the Summer so we spent a few days hiking in the area to look for and study them.'

'So they're like the mountain sheep in Wales?'

Rose laughed. 'A little yes. Both animals are tougher than their sea level counterparts but the ibex are a little more graceful. They have an amazing story too.'

Alex glanced at her again in the mirror, and Jacob turned to listen.

'Go on,' he said, seeing a flash of reticence on her face. 'We've got a three hour drive and I want to be an ibex expert by the time we arrive.'

She often got carried away talking about wildlife and geography and she was self-conscious about it after an ex-boyfriend of hers had criticised her for it, joking that she loved to hear the sound of her own voice. It had hurt her at the time, and still did, dampening her passion for all manner of things. But Jacob's sincere invitation for her to keep going had made her feel safe and she smiled and leant forward.

'Ok, so the Alpine ibex were once hunted, practically to extinction by the rural population for meat and for their horns, and by the middle of the 19th century there were less than a hundred remaining. We're talking poaching taking place over four hundred years, so it wasn't overnight, but the impact was huge. So King Victor the Second, of Italy, established a wildlife reserve around the remaining ibex, and employed over one hundred and fifty of his hunters to protect the species from poachers.'

Rose, still a little hesitant to go on, saw that Alex was looking at her again in the rear view mirror.

'Is that how they survived?' he said.

'It helped, the population recovered to a few hundred and the King allowed controlled hunting to resume but they weren't wild, not truly, and they were gone from the Alps entirely.'

'So how did they end up back here?' said Jacob.

'That's the exciting part. The Swiss government spent years trying to negotiate with the Italian royalty for a breeding pair to try and restore the population across the Alps, but in 1906 they ran out of patience and so the Swiss sent a group of poachers on a secret mission across the border to steal three baby ibex and return them alive. They were successful, and a hundred years later estimates suggest that there are now upwards of forty-five thousand ibex living across the alps and every single one of them can be traced back to those three babies stolen from the King's private hunting grounds. Isn't that incredible?'

Jacob nodded. 'That's nuts, some proper espionage. So do you think we'll see some on this trip?'

'Most likely, they're quite prevalent, although it depends on how high up we go. They tend to live above the timber line, but at this time of year some of them make their way down the slopes in groups to graze near the lakes, and as I said about Pontresina, some are brave or socialised enough to come right into the villages and towns. They are such beautiful animals.'

Rose felt a little embarrassed at her passion for the creature, but she found the story of the ibex inspiring and exciting and she longed to be involved in a conservation project that carried the weight and importance that those poachers must have felt all of those years ago.

'I'm sorry, I'm rambling,' she said. 'I want to hear about you guys.'

'What would you like to know?' said Alex.

'For starters, what have you been doing for three years?'

'Actually we've been meaning to tell you something,' said Alex, serious all of a sudden. 'We have a confession to make.'

Rose's stomach flipped and her heart seemed to start pounding harder in her chest. She sat upright and frowned.

'We're in love,' said Alex, grinning and leaning across to take Jacob's hand affectionately. 'After three years of living together, we've finally accepted who we are. We're gay men, Rose and we love one another and we do each other up the bum every night.'

Jacob burst out laughing pushing Alex's hand away as his friend tried to keep a straight face, but moments later he erupted into laughter too.

Rose tried to hide her relief as she realised Alex was joking.

'I always knew,' she said, loudly. 'I mean I literally spent years trying to shag one or the both of you, and you never showed the slightest bit of interest.'

The laughter slowed down as Alex looked in the rear view mirror again and Jacob glanced awkwardly at his friend.

'I'm joking boys, come on, give me some credit,' she said, trying to divert them away from her outburst of honesty. 'So come on, other than each other, what have you really done for the past three years?'

'Studied hard, of course,' said Alex. 'I hope I don't hear doubtful implication in your voice, young Prim?'

She smiled. 'Of course not, I assumed you'd both been

good boys. But come on. Girls? Adventures? Conquests? Trips? So much must have happened.'

'It wasn't as fun without you,' said Jacob.

Rose felt a sudden and deep sense of guilt, and looked out of the window.

'Ouch, that hurts dude, I'm right here,' said Alex, pretending to admonish his friend, but he knew it was true too.

She smiled, feeling a small blush rising up from her neck. She breathed in deeply to mask it.

'Let's start with family then,' said Rose. 'How's your mum and dad?' she said, aiming the question at Jacob who had turned to look at her.

There was an awkward silence as Alex looked across at his friend.

'Don't wind me up, again,' said Rose, concerned.

Jacob smiled kindly. 'I'm not, I'm sorry Rose. Dad passed away last year.'

'Oh gosh, I'm so sorry Jacob,' she leaned forward reaching for his hand and taking it in hers.

'It's okay,' he said squeezing her fingers gently. 'It was a heart attack, his lifestyle was always going to catch up with him. I got to say goodbye though.'

'Oh shit, I'm so sorry,' she said, closing her hand firmly around his. Alex glanced down once or twice as their fingers entwined. 'How's your mum doing?'

'Surprisingly well, she loved Dad but him passing away has meant she can get out again, she's joined a few clubs, started learning to salsa. She's actually pretty good,' he laughed. 'Her and a friend are entering a competition next month.'

'Is Olivia okay?' said Rose. She and Jacob's little sister had never got on. 'Is she well?'

'Well enough. She struggled at first but she's got a fairly

serious boyfriend now and they moved in together a few months back. You might remember him, actually, Adam Chapman? He was in our year at college.'

'The guy who had all the snakes?' said Rose, shocked.

'That's the guy,' said Jacob laughing.

'How the hell did they meet?'

'I'm not quite sure, and I don't think I ever want to find out,' said Jacob, releasing Rose's hand. She leaned back into her seat again and looked out the window at the beauty of Lake Geneva down in the valley to the south as another plane banked and dipped on approach to the airport, the low sun reflecting off the fuselage as it rolled.

Jacob's dad had treated her like one of the family and she was sad to hear he had passed away. She always felt like he'd treated her like a daughter, which may have been why Olivia hated her so much. She thought back to the time just a few years ago, when she had drunkenly called him by mistake from a party and asked for a lift home, and instead of admonishing her or telling her to call her own parents, he had dressed and driven for over an hour, at well past midnight, to come and collect her and deliver her safely home. He had been kind and caring, just like Jacob. The apple had not fallen far from the tree.

'What about you Alex?' she said, hesitant to ask about his family directly.

'Mum's as bonkers as ever. She's dating some guy who's part of a biker gang these days, so I don't see her much. Dad's brought a plot of land with Sally over by Hastings, he's got some grand idea of building his own house now he's retired.'

'Does he understand the concept of retirement?' laughed Rose.

'Pretty sure he didn't get the memo,' said Alex, shaking his head.

'Do you remember when we stole their garden gnomes?'

she said, laughing.

'Oh shit, yes. Sally was furious,' he said, hitting the steering wheel with the palm of his hand. 'They were searching for weeks for them. We hid them in so many other gardens.'

'The one on top of Mrs Soubry's roof is still there,' said Jacob.

'No fucking way,' said Rose. 'I nearly died getting down from there, Alex had to catch me before I fell through the greenhouse.'

'It's still there, looking down from the roof,' said Jacob.

'I am so proud. We were professional mischief makers.'

Rose sat back in her seat again, smiling.

As she closed her eyes, she was starting to think she was glad she'd come.

Her head back on the rest, she let a wave of nostalgia sweep over her, and did her best not to think about the days, and weeks and months that followed her decision to move away from the boys. How she hadn't eaten, or slept properly, the anxiety and the nervousness. How she'd cried herself to sleep at night for weeks, missing them both. How hard she had worked and how much it had affected her to slowly, carefully and surely cut them out of her life, for her own good.

But most of all, she tried not to think about how much it had hurt her and broken her heart.

Now here she was, burying the fear in the back of her mind that these three days could be a huge mistake that would plunge her headlong into a dark place that she had no desire to return to.

As she repressed her fears, she focused on the positives.

She was in Switzerland.

She was going climbing, hiking and wild camping.

She was with two men that she would always trust with

her life. And despite everything she had tried to do to change it, she loved them both dearly.

The biggest change of all though, was that they had all grown up.

She sighed and smiled.

This was going to be a great few days.

*

CHAPTER THREE

Alex pulled the car into the car park and as he gently rolled to a stop, Rose woke up.

She didn't want to open her eyes at first, but as she did she glanced up just in time to see Jacob look away. She smiled, wondering if he'd been watching her sleep. In many ways he was quite fraternal towards her, and had always acted like a big bear of a brother, protective and a little overbearing, even possessive at times and it was comforting to see that he still felt like that. He was an actual big brother to his little sister after all, so it came naturally to him, but it seemed a little different now. Although that might just have been wishful thinking on her part.

There were just a few other vehicles parked in the small car park as Jacob opened his door and stepped out into the warm sun. He stretched and jumped up and down on the spot before opening Rose's door and holding out his hand for her to step out. She took it gracefully and blushed a little as he pulled her up and out of the seat with an understated strength. She was more than capable of getting out of a car by herself and if it had been anyone else giving her the delicate little flower routine they would have received an earful by now, but Rose was finding it hard to resist his charming and gentle manner.

Alex had bounced out of the drivers seat and was now stood looking around with wide eyed amazement at the grandeur of the scenery that surrounded them on all sides. She admired and shared his passion.

'Isn't it stunning?' she said as she stood next to him.

'Beautiful,' he said quietly as he glanced over at her.

Jacob opened the boot of the car and began to unload their rucksacks onto the gravel floor, then he looked over at the two of them standing side by side and walked over to join them. For a few moments they all stood quietly together, enjoying the view. Rose reached out either side of her and took their hands in her own.

'Thank you,' she said.

Alex turned to look at her. 'What for?'

'For organising this and inviting me,' she said. 'And for being my friends.'

'Stop being mushy, Prim, you'll make Jacob cry.'

She laughed. 'I mean it though, it means so much to me to be out here with you both. Your friendship got me through school and college, and... I'm sorry I ran way, I just-'

'It's okay,' she felt Jacob squeeze her hand softly. 'You're here now.'

Rose wiped away a tear and withdrew her hands from the both of them.

'Yes, you're right. Sorry, I'm just overwhelmed. Fuck,' she laughed. 'This place is beautiful.'

'Are you ready?' said Jacob.

Rose looked around, slowly taking in the view, and

committing it to memory.

'Yes,' she said. 'Hell yes.'

'Let's do this,' said Alex and with that he grabbed Rose by the waist and hoisted her up onto his shoulder, holding her firmly there as she screamed and pounded his back with her fists. He threw the keys to Jacob and shouted across the carpark.

'You grab the bags mate, I'll bring her.'

Jacob laughed and walked over to the back of the car, pulling the boot closed. He locked it and stowed the key in his pocket, and then strapped Rose's bag to his chest, looping one arm through each of the other two bags and setting off in the direction of the arch which marked the start of the trail.

'You look like a donkey mate,' said Alex turning back as he marched Rose across the carpark.

'How appropriate,' said Jacob. 'You look like an ass.'

'Put me down, you caveman,' shouted Rose, still laughing but starting to feel a little heavy headed. As Alex reached the starting point, he placed her gently down on a high rock, her feet dangling over the edge.

'My lady,' he said politely and bowed, stepping back from her.

Rose's hair was tussled, her face was bright red and she felt flustered and a little winded. She jumped down from the rock and scooped up her bag.

'You're such a dick,' she said as she walked past him and then broke into a run. 'Race you to the tree,' she shouted as she took off.

'Oh no you don't,' said Alex breaking into a sprint and chasing after her.

Jacob watched, arms raised in frustration as Alex left his bag on the ground by Jacob's feet and sped after their friend, dust rising up from his shoes in a small cloud.

As Jacob caught up with them both, he found Rose leaning

against the tree, laughing and smiling and it reminded him of all the times they would play together out on the field during lunch breaks, making up silly games, racing each other, kicking a ball around, and then later, just hanging out together and talking and laughing.

He longed to be back there.

All the time he was at school he was desperate to leave, to move on and grow up and be an adult. Now he was there, at the start of his career, a bright future ahead of him, and he found he wanted nothing more than to go back to the days of school where he was carefree and young and do it all again. Although he'd do a few things differently.

He'd have kissed Rose for one.

As Rose caught her breath, she said, 'So what next Mr Neanderthal? You going to hit me over the head and take me back to your cave?'

'Later,' said Alex, smirking. 'For now,' he said as he reached for his backpack, still dangling from Jacob's arm. 'We're walking south for three kilometres and heading up around four hundred metres, walking in that direction.' He pointed and smiled.

Rose raised her eyebrows. 'Let's get moving then.'

The first part of the trail was easy going, it was a gentle ascent along a wide path that had been etched into the base of a sheer rock face running parallel to a deep gorge. The drop off to the right was steep and it felt quite dizzying walking above the trees which were swaying in the breeze down below them.

Alex was taking the lead and Jacob was bringing up the rear, with Rose in between the two, feeling safe and well looked after. Jacob wasn't complaining either, he had a good view after all. Rose's leggings didn't leave much to the imagination.

Again she thought to herself that if she had been here with

anyone else she would've taken self-righteous offence over their masculine protective behaviour, but with the two men it was just natural, for them and for her. She was also consciously enjoying adding a little extra sway to her hips as she walked.

Ahead of them the path continued across a short footbridge with a handrail that circumvented a spectacular waterfall. A fine sheen of mist contained a rainbow of colours which turned and sparkled and warped as they drew near. The sight and the sound of the water crashing past and falling down hundreds of metres into the river below was thunderous and awe inspiring.

For several minutes they all stood on the bridge, marvelling up towards the source and down into the dizzying depths of the gorge. Rose's knuckles turned white as she held on tight to the hand rail and leaned over the edge, feeling a keen sense of vertigo as she did.

By the time they reached the other side they each had a fine layer of fresh cool water covering their skin, and their clothes were permeated, but it was revitalising in the warm midday sun.

'I'm soaked,' said Rose, wiping a layer of water off her face.

'Do you remember that water park we visited in the sixth form?' said Alex.

'Crazy Canyon?' laughed Rose, screwing up her face at him, knowing what was coming.

'That's the one,' said Alex, almost doubling over with laughter. Jacob shook his head from side to side as he walked.

'I haven't forgotten,' said Rose. 'It's kind of hard to forget accidentally showing off my tits to half of our year group.'

'All I remember is Jacob trying to cover you up with his jacket, and everyone booing. What even happened?'

'You don't remember?'

'I saw tits, I didn't much care how or why at the time.'

'You're so fucking shallow,' laughed Rose. 'I was wearing a sports bra and a t-shirt as I knew I was going to get soaked, so mum had suggested I wear them to avoid looking like I'd been taking part in some rude competition. The ride had those shoulder bars that came down on a mechanical arm and clipped together between your legs. Well the bar came down and clamped over the edge of my t-shirt but I didn't know. When the ride finished, my top got stuck, so when the bar came up, my t-shirt came with it, and somehow the bra stuck to it. The only way I could get out without being hung, was to slip out of both.'

Alex had stopped as he was laughing too hard. 'That's amazing. I didn't even know that was possible.'

'Jacob here, was a kind gentleman and gave me his jacket to preserve my modesty.'

'Too late, half the sixth form were queuing for the ride,' said Alex. 'You had a great pair of tits though.'

'Still do, thank you,' said Rose.

'Not seen them in four years,' said Alex, shrugging. 'Things change.'

'Well maybe I'll treat Jacob to a show later, and reward him for his gentlemanly behaviour.'

Alex laughed again. Was it her imagination though, or had what she'd just said got to him in some way. He had laughed, but it seemed less genuine.

'No need, Rose. I was happy to help.'

'Spoken like a true gentleman,' said Rose.

'A true gentleman never gets to see any tits,' said Alex.

They soon came to a brief halt as the ascent became trickier, zig-zagging up through a jagged crevice, just a hundred feet up, but a daunting challenge none-the-less.

Alex didn't appear to be fazed at all, stepping up quickly and hauling himself up onto the first step. Rose, not wanting to be outdone, but a little more concerned about her safety, swung her bag down, rummaged inside and produced a pair of fingerless gloves with a reinforced palm.

Out of the three, Rose was by far the most experienced climber and she wasn't going to miss an opportunity to prove herself. Especially to the boys.

In a flash she was up and standing next to Alex, her limber form gracefully ascending with speed from the ground. Without waiting for Jacob, she began to climb up onto the next jut, leaning forward, conscious of her heavy rucksack changing her centre of gravity.

She was fast, and Jacob admired it, and he could see that she was enjoying the thrill as she straddled the funnel which took them up to next part of the trail. Rose was now halfway up, and still gaining speed. Her slender arms and powerful calf muscles propelled her up the cliff side with little effort.

He found it dizzying.

Alex was around fifteen feet above him now as he began to climb beyond the first step, pulling his weight up with more effort than it took the others.

Rose called down from above.

'Do you remember us climbing in Devon on that residential trip?'

'When you dropped me on the support line?' said Jacob.

'The line was slack,' she said, protesting.

'It wasn't slack, you were distracted by Alex pointing out Mike Perry's arse crack,' said Jacob.

Alex burst into laughter. 'Oh shit, I remember, you fell thirty foot and hit the floor like a sack of potatoes. That must've hurt.'

'Damn right it did, I ended up walking back with Mrs Silver so I didn't have to climb back up the same way again. Took me an hour. I never got you back for that.'

'Looks like you're about to miss your chance again,' said

Rose.

'You wait until I get up there,' said Jacob, speeding up.

'What're you going to do? Punish me?' said Rose as she pulled herself up onto the brow, slipping on a loose rock scree with her foot as she did so.

'Look out,' shouted Alex as Jacob looked up.

A small shower of rocks and pebbles tumbled down the side of the rock face, gathering speed and creating a small land slip heading straight for the two men.

Alex side stepped and clung to a short ledge, his feet searching and scraping for grip as the rocks fell past him. Jacob however, had no choice but to cling on and lower his head beneath a thin outcrop.

The stones rained down around him bouncing off his shoulders and back and threatening to dislodge his handhold as several cracked against his knuckles.

As the noise subsided and the rock fall slowed, Rose leaned over the edge.

'Oh my gosh, Jacob?' Rose called out. 'Are you okay? Is he okay?'

From her position, Rose could see Alex but there was no sign of Jacob.

'Where is he, I can't see him? Jacob?' she called out again.

Alex found a footing and pulled himself up, shimmying back round until he was safely on the ledge, but Jacob was gone.

Moving quickly he lowered himself down and out of sight from Rose, peering below him.

'I'm okay,' came Jacob's voice as his friend came into view again.

Rose sat back hard and held her chest. Her eyes were filled with panic, and she was breathing hard.

'Just a few bumps and scrapes,' came Jacob's voice, laughing. 'When I get up there, you are in so much trouble,'

Now she started to laugh too.

'Is that a promise?' she shouted back.

'You bet your ass,' said Jacob. 'I'm coming for you.'

*

As the two men pulled themselves up over the brow of the ridge, Rose rushed forward and took their hands, pulling them up and onto their feet.

As Jacob stood she threw her arms around him as tight as she could.

'I'm so sorry,' she said. 'My foot slipped and I was rushing and it was stupid.'

'It's fine,' said Jacob, patting her on the shoulder as he pulled away. 'No harm done to me, but *you* on the other hand, are in extreme danger.'

A look of confusion crossed Rose's face but then she grinned, her eyes wide with excitement and fear.

'I'll give you a head start,' he said and then winked.

'What do you mean?' she said, stepping backwards, her arms out.

'I think he's telling you to start running,' said Alex.

'No, no, no. What are you going to do?' she said, backing away and turning around, holding up her hands in surrender, but it was too late. Jacob started to run towards her.

She broke into a sprint as she laughed, but he was too fast and he caught her in a matter of seconds, lifting her up into the air by her waist and tickling her. She screamed and laughed and writhed in his grip as he brought her down onto the grassy floor.

Then all of a sudden, Jacob wasn't in control. Rose had her arm around his neck and then his legs gave way and he was on his back. She had both of his wrists in her grip, twisted above his head and she was just inches from his face, one knee in his groin and a wicked smile on her face.

For a few seconds they were frozen, looking into each others eyes.

'Oh shit,' came Alex's voice. 'She got you good man.'

Rose was panicking, she hadn't meant to take him down quite so hard, or humiliate him, but her instincts had kicked in. Now she was worried that he might feel emasculated, but at the same time, it had felt good to dominate him.

He could feel her breath on his face, and for a brief second he looked down at her lips. A lock of her hair fell loose from her ear and tickled his forehead. Rose blew it away with a quick puff and then pecked him on the cheek.

As she loosened her grip he pounced, rolling her over onto her back and pinning her down. She suddenly found herself completely at his mercy. She couldn't move her arms or her hips, she tried to kick her legs up but they wouldn't budge.

She loved it.

'Touché,' she said, laughing as he let go.

He stood up and extended his hand down to her, helping her up from the floor and she did her best not to squeal as his strong arm pulled her up easily. The two of them locked eyes again and for a brief second she saw something predatory, as though he *wanted* her. It was forceful and full of desire and then it burned away and her friend was back in front of her.

Turning away, a little dazed and very turned on, she plucked up her rucksack and swung it onto her back again and then turned to see Alex looking drawn and a little deflated. He smiled and started heading off up the trail.

'If you two are done flirting, then we need to get moving.'

Jacob gestured for her to go first, the gentleman had returned, and although she loved this version of him, she wanted passionate and angry Jacob back again.

If only for half an hour.

Ten minutes passed by as the trio continued walking up

the hill toward what Rose was starting to suspect was a high altitude mountain lake. The ground was flat and wide here with a gentle incline and it was gradually becoming more wet and boggy as they neared the brow. Rose started to walk a little faster in her excitement, moving ahead of the pair of them and wondering to herself if either one (or both of them) were watching her as she moved.

She saw the lake before the two men, excitedly pressing on ahead as they all drew near.

It was ice blue and crystal clear.

Fed by glacial streams and meltwater run off, it was bound to be ice cold too, but that wasn't going to faze her.

As she approached the small beach that ran along the eastern shoreline, she dropped her rucksack and removed her shoes, kicking them off as she walked.

Jacob and Alex, still a little way back, found they were suddenly being treated to the sight of Rose stripping down to her underwear as they crested the brow, her clothes abandoned in a line heading down the beach. They watched in astonishment as she ran, just fast enough so she that didn't have time to change her mind. With no hesitation, she dove straight into the freezing cold waters of the lake, and went under.

As the pair watched, she re-emerged, her hair slicked back, her skin glistening, her eyes wide as she took a sharp, shocked breath and shivered violently.

'Oh shit,' she shouted. 'Shit, shit, shit it's cold.'

She breathed in, shuddering, and held her breath then dunked back under again. As she broke the surface once more, she swam towards them until she could put her feet down on the soft bed. The water was as clear as a window and below her she could see beautiful smooth pebbles, tiny fish and a sunken log brimming with life as she paddled.

The two men weren't hiding the fact that they were staring

at her and she laughed.

'You look like you've never seen me in my knickers before,' she shouted. 'Come on, get in, the waters… invigorating.'

'You didn't really sell it to us with the *shit, shit, shit* routine,' said Alex.

She could see that Jacob was already putting down his rucksack though, and not to be outdone, Alex quickly threw his down too.

Rose suddenly found herself in a difficult position. She wanted to watch the men strip down to their underwear and stride into the water, preferably in slow motion, but if she stared for too long she might come across as a little obvious and weird.

She decided to take the surreptitious approach and swim around a little, glancing back now and again and feeling more than a little excited.

As Alex removed his top however, Rose had to stop. He really had been hitting the gym. He was toned, muscular and broad and she couldn't help but stare.

Jacob noticed and a little pang of jealously had stung somewhere in his heart. Alex was more muscular than he was, but he was proud of his own body and had worked hard for it over the last two years. He stood up now and peeled off his own shirt, feeling the bracing wind on his skin, coming off the surface of the water as it rippled across the lake. He looked at Rose and could see that her attention was drawn to him now.

'Oh shit, I really am in trouble,' she whispered to herself as both men walked with purpose and poise into the water, and began swimming out to join her.

'Fuck,' said Alex as he got closer. 'Why is it so cold?'

'It's a glacial lake,' said Rose. 'It's also fed by meltwater from the ice above the snow line.'

Alex dunked his head under the water and came back up.

As he did so, Rose splashed him.

'Don't start something you can't finish, Prim.'

She raised her eyebrows in challenge. 'Is that what you think, Alex?' She splashed him again and as she did he erupted out of the water and grabbed her, pulling her down with him beneath the surface.

Moments later they came back up for air but Rose splashed him again, and then Jacob too, for good measure, before turning and swimming away towards the middle of the lake.

Jacob took off after her in pursuit. He was a powerful swimmer but she was light, so they were a fairly even match but Jacob had the edge and before long she felt his grip on her foot pulling her back. They grappled together for a moment, laughing and pushing one another as they tread water in the crystal clear turquoise that surrounded them.

It was surreal. As though they were floating fifty feet in the air, the bottom of the lake teeming with life, fish, sunken driftwood and rocks.

Rose reached out and took Jacob's hand beneath the water, interlinking his fingers with hers and holding tight as they floated together.

Jacob was finding it hard to keep his eyes from looking down into the water at Rose's body, but then something behind her distracted him.

It was Alex.

He erupted from behind Rose and grabbed her with both arms, pulling her back under again as she screamed. He let go of her hand as the pair of them disappeared and he watched them beneath the surface, tussling and turning. Then they were back up again, laughing and breathing deep.

As they wiped their eyes, Rose's expression changed to surprise and wonder and she pointed.

'Look, over there,' she said.

The two men followed her gaze and saw that just down the

shoreline from where they had entered the lake, was a small group of goat like animals which had ventured down to the waters edge for a drink.

'Ibex,' said Rose, whispering.

One of the ibex was looking towards them alert whilst the others drank.

Rose put a hand on Alex's shoulder to keep him still, feeling the muscles rippling beneath as he kept himself afloat.

One of the other ibex stopped lapping at the water and stepped back and another took its place as the first kept watch on the three humans, and then after another minute or so they started moving on, occasionally looking back to the middle of the lake to make sure they were still safe.

'They're so majestic,' said Rose, in awe.

Alex turned to her and smiled and then she felt Jacob's hand on her back.

'Come on, we best get out before we freeze.'

They swam calmly back to the beach together, Rose occasionally dipping under to look down below at the bottom of the lake, marvelling at how clear it was.

As they stepped out into the warm sun, Jacob opened his rucksack and removed a neatly folded bamboo microfibre towel and wrapped it around Rose's shoulders.

'What about you?' she said, shivering.

'I've got plenty of t-shirts,' he said and pulled out a loose one to start wiping himself down with.

Rose stood warming herself up and drying off whilst watching the ibex herd in the distance as it disappeared from view. She was so happy to see them again, and she was deep in thought about her future life and what shape it might take, working with inspirational animals like these, in awe inspiring environments like this.

She couldn't help but notice though, that both Jacob and Alex kept stealing glances at her standing there in her underwear as they dressed.

As the ibex disappeared from view, Rose unwrapped herself from the towel and gathered up her clothes. The two men were sat side by side on a rock, looking out over the lake, but she knew they were idly watching her too as she dressed. She bent down to pull on her leggings in front of them, smiling to herself as she did so. When she turned around she found they were both looking up into the mountains, pretending not to have been watching.

'You ready, Prim?' said Alex as she finished wringing out her hair and retying her ponytail.

'How far is it to camp?' she said, nodding.

'About three kilometres, not far at all.'

'Let's go then, perverts,' she said and set off grinning, without looking back.

*

The area that the boys had picked out for their camp was ideal, and Rose had to admit that she was impressed. The tree line acted as a natural wind break and the surrounding land was shaped like a crater so it provided shelter on almost all sides. They wouldn't even be visible from the path, making it completely private.

Alex arrived first and set down his rucksack.

'Home, sweet, home,' he said, gesturing his arms out in a circle and smiling.

'It's perfect,' said Rose.

Now she was here, Rose suddenly felt a strange mixture of vulnerability and exhilaration. Not only was she wild camping in the Swiss Alps, but she was up here with her two closest friends. She was also completely alone. There was no one else around for miles. She trusted them both completely but her wellbeing was entirely in their hands. It was also more than a little arousing.

She wanted desperately to push them both, to tease and be suggestive and drop hints of what she wanted them to do to her, but that wasn't right. She wanted them to want her, and she was beginning to think that maybe they did. She closed her eyes and pictured it for just a second and then stopped herself before she got carried away.

Alex threw his rucksack onto the floor and undid the buckles, releasing the rolled up tent he had neatly attached to the bottom. Jacob joined him and they began to unpack it, removing the poles, placing the pegs aside and unrolling the inner and outer. Rose leant back against a rocky outcrop and folded her arms to watch.

'You planning on helping at all or you just going to stand there admiring the view?' said Alex.

'Men at work,' said Rose, raising her eyebrows. 'It's quite the mesmerising experience.'

'Get your lazy ass over here and start hammering some pegs,' said Alex.

'Yes sir,' said Rose, pushing away from the rock.

She scooped up the mallet and worked her way around as the two men pushed the poles through the canvas and positioned it on the second most comfortable and flat surface they could find. The ground was soft and the pegs went in easily, occasionally finding a hard rock or two beneath the surface.

Once the larger tent was up, Jacob peeled away and left her and Alex to put up her smaller one person tent as he began to dig a small fire pit and gather some nearby wood. Rose found the sight of him using the small woodcutters axe to fell a few saplings and then a small tree rather distracting and Alex was noticing.

As the light began to fade Alex lit the fire using his magnesium flint striker, laying down low to stoke the flames with long slow breaths.

Whilst Alex got the fire going, Jacob invited her to help him drag over a few large logs for them to sit on and before long they were comfortable and cozy around the fire, warming themselves in the flames as the wheel of starlight began to swing above them.

Jacob had boiled up some water and made her a hot chocolate and she sipped at it whilst staring into the embers.

'So what about girls?' said Rose.

Alex looked over at Jacob and grinned.

'What about them?' he said, laughing.

Rose raised her eyebrows. 'Anyone pining after either of you at home?'

'Several girls, but no one I'm missing if that's what you're getting at?'

'Oh okay, Mr Player,' she laughed. 'I see how it is. You're a regular Romeo these days?'

'I do well,' said Alex, grinning at her and winking slowly.

'That doesn't work on me,' she laughed. She would never admit to him that it had.

'You wait,' he said, biting his lip.

'Oh my goodness, does this really work on girls, Jacob?' said Rose, gesturing at Alex.

'Unfortunately, almost every time.'

'I despair,' she said, aware and almost annoyed that she was now intensely aroused. 'So what about you Jacob? Are you charming the intellectual pants off any post-graduate psychology majors?'

'Not at the moment,' he said, more reserved than Alex.

'Don't hold back,' she said. 'There must have been someone special over the last three years?'

Rose knew full well that there had been, Jacob's profile pictures included several taken with his arm around a gorgeous red head.

'Mollie, Mollie, Mollie, Mollie!' said Alex, laughing.

Jacob smiled and looked down. 'There was Mollie,' said Jacob, nodding.

'Was?' said Rose, secretly hopeful.

'Was. We broke up two months ago.'

'She broke his heart,' said Alex and feigned stabbing himself with a knife in the chest. 'It was brutal, Prim.'

'It was a mutual decision,' said Jacob, calmly but still smiling.

'She shagged a bartender named Tanner,' whispered Alex.

Rose's eyes widened and she burst into laughter, then held her hand over her mouth in shock. 'No, really?'

Jacob nodded. 'I never said who the mutual decision was between.'

'Oh my goodness,' said Rose. 'You poor thing.'

'Don't feel too bad for him, she was just the runner up in the Rose look-a-like competition.'

Jacob looked sharply at Alex, admonishing him but his friend just shrugged back.

'What do you mean?' she said, puzzled.

'Alex,' said Jacob, trying to stop him.

'I mean,' he said. 'That Mollie, was the consolation prize in the Stunning Scottish Redhead Race.'

Alex winked at her as she frowned.

'He's winding you up,' said Jacob.

Rose knew what Alex meant, she wasn't stupid. But she was also hoping he wasn't winding her up.

'What about you?' said Jacob. 'Is there someone special up in Wales?'

Rose shook her head. 'Not for a little while now,' she said. 'I haven't really felt like dating much, I've just been focused on work and studies. I kind of wish my flat mate would think the same way sometimes and stop shagging about, but that's another story.'

'I would like to meet your flat mate,' said Alex, leaning forward.

'She would love you,' laughed Rose, but her head was preoccupied, thinking about what Alex had said before about Jacob.

Mollie was the consolation prize, those were the words he had used.

Interesting.

As the fire died down over the course of the evening, the three of them began to tire and Jacob was the first to turn in, saying goodnight to them both and crawling into the three person tent that both he and Alex would be sleeping in for the next few nights.

Alex and Rose sat together for a little longer, both staring into the fire, seeing shapes, shadows and visions in the flames. Rose found it mesmerising.

'I'm sorry if I was a dick earlier,' said Alex.

Rose frowned and turned to look at him.

'When?' she said.

'About the water park,' said Alex, still looking into the fire.

'That's okay,' said Rose.

'I just get carried away around you.'

Rose blushed and looked back into the fire.

'Sorry,' said Alex. 'I don't have Jacob's way with words. I'm not a poet. I'm just glad you're here.'

Rose flashed a smile. Then she reached out and took his hand in hers, interlocking his fingers. Her hand felt tiny inside his.

Neither of them spoke for a while, but both of their minds were racing. After a few minutes, Alex turned to look at her face, the flames dancing on her skin.

'Do you think… if I'd, said something, back then?'

'Yes,' said Rose, not waiting for him to finish.

Alex nodded and looked back into the dying embers, his

hand still clasped around hers.

After a while she let go, and stood up to head off towards her tent, pausing next to her old friend and placing her hand on his shoulder affectionately.

'Alex,' she said. 'Are you happy?'

He looked up at her and smiled.

'Now that you're back,' he said. 'Yes.'

*

Rose was cold and lonely.

She had been wild camping hundreds of times on her own. She loved the feeling of being away from the bustling towns and cities, away from the intensity of the University. Far from family and friends. Just a thin piece of nylon between her and the rest of the world, half way up a mountain. Whether she was knee deep in snow, being hammered by torrential rain, lighting, thunder, wind or the quiet stillness of a bright Summer's night. It didn't matter where she was, when she was alone, she was happy.

But now, with Alex and Jacob just ten feet away, she was lonely and desperately sad. She wanted to be back with them. So much so, that it hurt.

Everything about today had been perfect. It was as though the last three years hadn't happened. As though nothing had changed.

But that wasn't strictly true.

Something *had* changed but she wasn't quite sure she was ready to believe it. Both Jacob and Alex seemed to be vying for her attention, as though there was a little competition between them.

They had always been competitive, always intent on outdoing each other, but the competition had always been between them, not about her and now it seemed like the dynamic had shifted.

Absence makes the heart grow fonder, she thought.

That's how she felt right now.

Absent, as though she was missing.

Fuck.

She unzipped her sleeping bag and wriggled out of it then bundled it up into her arms. Trying her best to keep her head down low, she crawled to the end of her tent and opened the zip as quietly as she could and then turned around and backed out, slipping on her boots as she went.

The night was bright and filled with stars, just a few wisps of cloud here and there, scattered across a deep and beautiful sky.

Alex and Jacob's tent was just a few yards away, the guy ropes luminous and reflecting the starlight.

She wanted to be with them. Not in her own tent, like a third wheel or a spare part. They weren't fourteen and on a residential camping trip, barred from entering the boys tents, segmented by gender. They were adults, and she didn't want be alone, and they were her friends.

She wanted to be close to them.

Close enough to reach out and touch them.

She took a deep breath and walked over towards the thin, erect sheet of canvas that separated the three of them, clutching her sleeping bag as her heart pounded in her chest.

As quietly, and as slowly, and as gently as she could, she began to unzip the men's tent, but as she reached the halfway point she started to panic.

What was she thinking?

That she could just slide in between them without them noticing? Then wake up in the morning, like… Surprise! The whole impulsive idea seemed foolish now and she was overwhelmed with a sudden sense of shame and silliness.

She froze, her fingers still on the zipper.

'Rose?' came Alex's voice from inside the tent.

There was some shuffling and movement and then the inner fly sheet was opening and Alex's hand appeared. He fumbled for the zip and instead found Rose's fingers and for a brief moment he paused as they touched. Then he was unzipping the tent and looking up at her with a broad but quizzical smile.

'Everything okay?' he whispered. 'What's wrong?'

Rose didn't know what to say, so she said nothing at all.

Alex frowned and then saw the swaddled up sleeping bag in her arms. 'Do you want to come in?'

She nodded tentatively, and he smiled. It was such a disarming and friendly smile that she immediately felt as though she was eleven years old again and all her worries about school and making friends and being intimidated by the older children were fading away.

She knelt down and shuffled inside, pulling her sleeping bag in with her.

Jacob was still sleeping, so Alex shifted over and made a space for her between them and then lightly patted the groundsheet inviting her to come and lay down.

She rolled out her sleeping bag into the space and then realised that she had left her travel pillow back in her own tent. Alex saw her expression change and then looked around, turned over and came back with his jumper, bunching it up into a ball and tucking it inside the hood of her sleeping bag. He winked at her in the twilight and then lay back down as she wriggled in beside him, pulling the zip closed past her hips and snuggling down onto the make shift pillow.

She placed a hand on his shoulder and whispered.

'Thank you.'

He smiled back and closed his eyes and within a few

minutes he was gently snoring.

Now Rose had a different problem. She wasn't lonely anymore, and she wasn't cold. In fact she was warm and getting warmer by the second.

The smell of Alex's jumper was intoxicating. As subtly as she could, she buried her face in it and breathed in his scent, sensing a mixture of spice, wood and sweat. Her legs twitched.

She rolled over, away from Alex and found Jacob's closed eyes facing her, sleeping more quietly than his friend. She could feel his breath on her face, and she trembled as a few loose strands of her hair shifted as he exhaled.

She bit her lip and breathed in deeply, then closed her eyes and tried to calm herself down.

Here she was, miles from another person, but inches from the two men she loved more than anyone else in the world, and she was tucked between the two of them just like in one of her fantasies.

She couldn't help it. She was incredibly aroused, and her arousal was building by the second as her mind raced.

Her body shook with adrenaline as images flashed through her mind of the two men ravishing her inside the tent. Their bodies dripping with sweat and desire as they each fucked her in turn.

Oh shit, she thought as her lips went dry.

She was soaking wet already and her pussy was aching to be touched. She bit her lip again, hard enough to draw blood, but it was no good.

As slowly and as carefully as she could, she squeezed her legs together and started to gently rock her hips back and forth inside her sleeping bag. She realised she was holding her breath, and as softly as she could, she exhaled through her nose, trying to not breathe onto Jacob's brow, not wanting to disturb him or wake him up, but just to look upon his face.

She was going to do it.

It was a huge risk, but she had to, she couldn't take it any longer.

Trying to make as little noise as possible, she rolled onto her back, slid her hands down past her hips and tucked her thumbs into the sides of her leggings and her underwear. Then she arched her back and raised herself off the floor of the tent and in one slow and smooth motion she pulled both garments down around six inches until they were resting beneath the curve of her bottom.

Just the sheer act of removing her underwear, so close to Jacob and Alex had her whole body quivering and close to climax.

She stayed still and silent, holding her breath again and listening intently, shaking and so incredibly turned on by what she was doing that she was worried she might orgasm the moment she touched herself.

The boys remained asleep.

She moved her head ever so slightly to look across at Alex, and then back over to Jacob. One last check. Then she moved her hand down, sliding her knuckles under the soft material lining of the sleeping bag. She parted her soft lips and twitched as the tip of her finger brushed against her clit, and then she began to circle herself, excruciatingly slowly.

She'd never felt like this before, never touched herself like this. The fear of being caught by either one of them was like an adrenaline rush of arousal. She didn't want to breathe for fear of being discovered, but the idea that one of them might wake up and roll over and see what she was doing was a turn on too.

She tried not to make a sound as her finger continued to make a circle, doing her best to avoid brushing against the sides of the sleeping bag for fear of making a rhythmic rustle that might rouse them.

In her mind she pictured them waking up, Alex opening his eyes and seeing her. Her head arched back, her hand between her legs. She could almost hear the noise of him unzipping her sack, throwing it aside and exposing her. Her fingers still inside herself. Then Jacob waking up too, and seeing her naked between them, trying to hide her modesty, trying in vain to pull up her leggings. Alex stopping her and putting his hand between her legs as Jacob leaned in and kissed her.

She put her hand on her own breast and squeezed, imagining it was Jacob as she quickened her pace. Then she let out an involuntary moan as she pictured Alex rolling her onto her front and parting her legs.

She thought of his dick resting on her ass, how big it would feel, and how hard.

The feeling of him pulling her up onto all fours.

Thrusting into her.

Filling her up.

She moaned.

Alex wriggled and she froze.

Then a second later he rolled over towards her.

Her eyes remained fixed, looking up at the roof of the tent and then ever so slowly she turned her head to look at him.

He was still asleep.

She took a stuttering deep breath and then turned away to exhale before starting again. Her mind going back to imagining herself vulnerable, warm, and naked between them.

On all fours.

Exposed.

The pair of them fucking her, one after the other. First Alex and then Jacob and then Alex again as Jacob filled her mouth.

Harder and harder.

Both of them cumming inside her.

Alex's seed in her pussy, warm and wet. Jacob's in her mouth.

She moaned again.

Jacob stirred beside her, beginning to wake. She panicked but then found she couldn't stop, it was too late.

The orgasm was quick and dirty and she twitched and shook, turning her head from side to side as it worked its way through her. She tried not to moan again or even breathe out and her vision filled with stars, floating in front of her likes motes of dust.

She felt a hand on her shoulder and jumped.

It was Jacob, and he was looking right at her.

'Rose, are you okay?' he whispered, gently shaking her shoulder. 'You're having a bad dream.'

Her skin was covered in a thin layer of sweat and the tent was dripping with condensation.

She breathed out, at last, shuddering as she did so, still not quite able to form words so she nodded and looked over towards Alex as she slipped her hand out from between her legs.

She left her underwear and leggings where they were. There was something naughty about talking to Jacob whilst she was secretly in an indecorous state.

'I'm okay,' she said.

He nodded and lay back down, still looking concerned.

She wanted to kiss him so much.

To tell him that she was touching herself and thinking of him.

Of them both.

But she couldn't, she didn't dare.

Not yet.

*

CHAPTER FOUR

The following morning, Rose woke up to find both Jacob and Alex awake, dressed and sat in the porch cooking breakfast. Outside the weather was wet and dreary and she could hear the wind whipping at the flaps of the tent.

'Something smell's amazing,' she said, sitting up, her sleeping bag still wrapped tightly around her. 'What are we having?'

'Bacon and eggs,' said Alex.

'Oh my goodness,' she said, laying back down. 'I'm in heaven.'

She started to laugh and the two men turned around to look at her.

'I'm on a mountain, in the Swiss Alps, and my two favourite men are making me bacon and eggs in bed,' she said with her eyes closed.

'There's a cup of coffee out here too,' said Jacob.

'I love you, I actually love you,' said Rose sitting back up again.

Jacob passed the warm insulated mug through to her and she took it in both hands.

She suddenly remembered that her knickers and leggings were still down around her knees and she blushed, hiding her face in the steam from the coffee.

'So, didn't fancy sleeping on your own last night then?' said Alex as she sipped.

She shook her head slowly and smiled. 'Bad dreams,' she said.

'What happened?' asked Jacob.

'It was my wedding day, and Alex was the groom,' she said, grinning.

'Oh wow, that's rough,' said Jacob. 'I'm surprised you're still here.'

Alex laughed and winked at her. 'If it had been our wedding *night* you wouldn't have *wanted* to wake up.'

'Ooh, how rude,' said Rose, then she shook her head and shrugged. 'Honestly I don't remember, I just woke up feeling scared and I didn't want to be alone.'

Jacob nodded. 'You can stay with us again tonight if you need to?'

'Maybe you can finish the dream?' said Alex, raising his eyebrows.

Rose took another sip of coffee and smiled, nodding gently.

'I'd like that,' she said, grinning at him.

Jacob stabbed his fork into the small frying pan and lanced a piece of bacon, dropping it onto a small camping plate next to a neatly fried egg. He passed it back to Rose who took it eagerly, setting aside her coffee.

She leant forward, forgetting that she hadn't adjusted herself before she fell asleep last night and in doing so exposed her breast.

Jacob faltered and nearly dropped the plate, eyes wide.

'Oh sorry, you, er-', he pointed as Rose looked at him confused, then she followed his gaze and gasped, pulling her top down swiftly, her face turning crimson.

'Oh my,' she said.

Alex's face appeared in the gap. 'What? What did I miss?' He looked at Jacob whose face was frozen with the slightest hint of a grin.

Rose started laughing and covered her face in shame. 'You missed boob, I'm afraid,' she said.

'What? That's not fair,' said Alex. 'You're dreaming about marrying me, but he gets to see your boobs?' He shook his head. 'I demand a replay.'

'No!' said Rose, laughing harder.

'Slow motion rewind?'

'No way!'

'Then I want a divorce,' he said, his head disappearing back into the porch. 'We're over, Prim.'

'I'm so embarrassed, I'm so sorry Jacob.'

'Don't be sorry, it was an accident,' he said, laughing as his own face regained its normal colour. 'A happy accident.'

Rose picked up a sock and threw it at him and he darted out of the way, disappearing into the porch with his friend.

She threw herself backwards and buried her face in Alex's jumper, sniffing it again as she did so.

'I'm just going to stay in here today,' she called out, still mortified but smiling. 'Don't really fancy it out there.'

Whilst she genuinely hadn't meant to expose herself, it had certainly had a desirable effect.

She opened her eyes briefly to check that the boys weren't looking and then shuffled her arms down inside the sleeping bag to pull up her knickers and leggings.

By the time she emerged, still somewhat embarrassed and feeling very awkward, the wind had begun to pick up and the visibility was dropping.

What had once been a stunning view of the snow tipped Alps was now just a mottled spread of dark and grey clouds.

The air felt damp too, and although it wasn't raining yet, it was threatening to do so.

Rose walked over to her abandoned tent and slipped inside to get changed as the two men began to pack and decamp and a few minutes later she emerged in full waterproofs, her hood shaped tightly around her face.

'Don't think there's any chance of any more happy accidents today, mate,' said Jacob as he watched Rose packing away her tent, wrapped up from head to toe.

After clipping the lightweight canvas bag onto the bottom of her rucksack, she hoisted it onto her shoulder, and then turned and smiled at the two men.

'So what's the plan today?'

Alex stood up, leaving the partially rolled up inner layer of their tent on the ground, pulled down his hood and beckoned her over.

He knelt on the grass and removed the map from his rucksack and then flattened it out on a fairly large piece of rock.

'I *was* thinking we could take this scramble up the side of here but I think it's going to be too dangerous now, especially if the rain comes in, so instead, we head down and round here and walk through the forest, which might give us a bit of shelter. Then we can head back up to tonight's camp,' he said as he pointed. 'If we cut up through this track here.'

'Could we go up and over instead?' said Rose.

Alex frowned and Rose leaned in to point.

'If we double back here and took this route up and over, then we might get to see an inversion, and then we can peak today too,' she shrugged. 'Depends on how high up the cloud cover is though.'

Jacob nodded. 'Works for me.'

Alex looked up at him, frowning. 'You saw boob this morning, I don't trust your judgment,' he said. 'But, it does seem like a good idea.'

Rose smiled.

'Tell you what Prim, if you promise to even the score,' said Alex, nodding toward Jacob. 'We'll go with your plan.'

Rose's eyes widened and she looked over at Jacob, shocked.

'I'm not getting involved,' he said, laughing.

'I'm not showing you my tits just to get my way.'

'Fine, woods it is,' said Alex, standing up.

Rose was incredulous, her eyes wide and her jaw open in astonishment.

'Fine. How about this? I *might* even the score later this evening, on the condition that I get to sleep in your tent again, and we go up and over, and I get another bacon sandwich and a coffee tomorrow morning?'

Jacob laughed. 'She drives a hard bargain.'

Alex feigned thinking about it as Rose stood, arms crossed and pouting.

'Just the one boob though,' she said. 'Not both.'

Alex laughed and smiled. 'Deal, but you do know I'm kidding don't you?'

Rose looked a little disappointed.

'I hope not,' she grinned. 'Come on, let's get going before the rain soaks your groundsheet. I'm sleeping in there tonight don't forget.'

The two men packed up quickly and stowed their gear, covering their own rucksacks in clip on waterproof outer shells as Rose helped.

As they began to leave the first rumble of thunder grumbled in the distance.

*

***

The rain was light at first. It felt like more of a mist than a shower and as the breeze grew in strength, Rose could see the fine drizzle drifting and forming shapes amongst the rocks. Ahead of her was the shrouded figure of Jacob, hunching forward as he stepped up onto a raised outcrop, slick with rainwater. Their path was becoming treacherous but Rose was used to it. She'd spent weeks, possibly months of the last three years on and around the mountains of Snowdonia. This part of their climb reminded her of Tryfan in the Ogwen Valley, an enjoyable but difficult climb in good weather, but lethal in the rain and wind.

She hoped they would peak before the weather caught up with them.

She paused to look back towards Alex, her knee bent up onto a ledge, one foot down and her hands splayed and gripping the rock face. He was thirty foot behind and below her, and although he was strong, his bulk was slowing him down.

'Do you need a hand?' she shouted into the wind, but there was no response.

She pulled herself up and steadied her feet as the wind whipped at her hood. She could hear the waterproof cover of her backpack working its way loose and she swung it down off her shoulder to tighten it.

When she stood back up she saw that Jacob had paused and was looking back down at her. He raised his thumb and she replied in kind and then turned back to look down at Alex again. He was closer now and seemed to be moving a little faster, perhaps spurred on by the increasingly poor weather.

Adjusting her rucksack she found a foothold and clambered up onto the next step. She was very appreciative of her waterproof boots, now they were being dunked into three inch deep rock pools every other step.

Jacob was waiting for her and as she approached she saw his expression.

'What's wrong?' she shouted over the noise of the rain battering her hood.

'I think we've gone wrong,' said Jacob. He nodded at the map in his hands. 'I think we should've come up this path here, but we've ended up too high.'

Rose studied the map as Alex caught up with them.

'We lost?' he said as he approached.

'A little,' said Jacob. 'We're too high, I think.'

Rose nodded in agreement.

'We can rejoin the path up ahead, but it looks like we have to cross a stream,' she said, handing the map back to Jacob. 'Or we go back down and find the intersection.'

'Cross the stream,' said Alex.

Rose nodded. 'Might be tough in this weather?'

Jacob shrugged. 'Beats going back down that way in the rain.'

Alex took the lead now, stepping ahead of the others and onto the narrow path before them. The wind was still gathering strength and as they began to walk, Rose tightened the hood around her face. In the distance, she heard another, much deeper rumble of thunder.

The stream was a few hundred meters ahead and as they approached, Rose wondered if they would have been better heading back. It was six foot wide, with only a narrow crossing and it barely contained the torrent of rushing water which was crashing down into it from the side of the mountain.

Alex arrived at the edge first, looking down into the mist below where the water disappeared and then up into the clouds above them. To cross they would have to first climb down into the eroded channel that the water had carved, and then carefully step across several boulders that had fallen into the path of the fall at some point or another and been pushed downstream.

Always the brave one, Alex slid down first. The side of the rock was smooth and as he reached the edge he struggled to find his footing, the power of the rushing water dislodging his feet wherever he placed them. Once he was steady, he looked back up and signalled for Rose to come down to him.

She nodded and then turned to face the wall, sliding the toes of her boots down on the rock face and lowering herself with Jacob's help. Alex took hold of her waist as she reached the bottom and steadied her, and she couldn't help but feel humbled by his strength. Finding her balance and a solid footing, she looked sideways at him as he caught her eye.

'You okay?' he said.

Rose nodded.

'I'm going to cross and then throw a rope back for you and Jacob,' he said. 'I seem to remember you're pretty good at catching.'

'The best,' said Rose, laughing.

There wasn't a lot of room between them and the torrent, and as Alex slid past he had to hold her waist tightly, pressing her into the rock face with his body.

Had he lingered longer than necessary? Or was it just her imagination?

She turned to watch as he started to cross, crouching down and holding onto a sharp outcrop with her fingers. She was so close to the stream now that the spray as it crashed past was making her squint.

Alex steadied himself and let go of the side, balancing momentarily and then swinging himself forward and onto the first boulder, spreading his weight and testing how steady the rock was before adjusting his centre of gravity and moving up and onto it fully.

He had nothing to hold onto now, so he crouched low before moving onto the second, lower rock which Rose could see was just an inch or two below the surface.

There was a bright flash of light and then a second later a deafening roar of thunder.

Rose jumped and nearly lost her footing, and for a moment she took her eyes off Alex. When she looked back, he was unbalanced. It was happening slowly, not in slow motion, but she could see that he was fighting to stop himself from falling into the torrent. His foot, now two inches into the current was being pushed off the rock, but his centre of gravity was too far over and he couldn't recover.

Rose watched in horror as Alex's foot slipped and he fell into the water. The current was carrying him down, and in that moment she reacted, reaching out and grabbing his arm as he tumbled past.

The muscles in her arm screamed in pain as she held on to the ledge, her fingers white hot as they dug in. Alex's fingers gripped her arm hard, crushing her as he held on. She felt movement beside her as Jacob slid down and then a moment later, he was hauling Alex back and pushing him against the side of the small gorge.

Her arm ached, but she didn't care.

She'd nearly lost him.

She choked back tears as she looked over at him, panting and staring up into the sky, a strange grin on his face. Part of her wanted to hug him, and the other part wanted to slap him.

'Oh shit, that was close,' he said. 'You're a life saver, Prim. I owe you one.'

'Damn right you do,' she said. She wanted to rub her arm but there was no way she was letting go of the ledge.

Jacob was moving now and had stepped over onto the large boulder from where Alex had fallen.

'Alex, pass me the rope,' said Jacob.

The rope was attached to the side of Alex's bag, looped and tethered with a carabiner. He unclipped it and slid it down and then threw Jacob one end whilst he tied the other around his waist.

'This would've been more sensible,' he said, grinning at Rose.

Jacob tied the other end around his own waist and then with much more confidence than Alex, he stepped down onto the submerged stone and then straight away stepped onto the next, a raised but slanted rock, just a foot from the other side. He deftly jumped and then turned and leaned back against the muddy hillside opposite.

'Take the slack,' he shouted and Alex complied, pulling the rope tight between them.

'Come on, Rose,' said Alex, beckoning to her.

Taking a deep breath, she stood back up and then made her way toward him carefully, leaning against the rock face and sliding along until she was beside him.

She took hold of the rope, closed her eyes and built up her courage and then jumped up onto the first rock, stepped down onto the second as she'd seen Jacob do, adjusted her balance, hopped to the third and then leapt across to Jacob, who caught her in his arms.

She stayed there for a moment, enjoying the embrace but then Alex was shouting to them.

'This is no time for a cuddle,' he said. 'Get me over there.'

Rose stepped aside as Jacob took the slack again, and she began to climb up and out of the small gully, digging her feet into the mud and sliding with each step.

When she reached the top, grabbing hold of tufts of grass to pull herself out, she turned around to see that both the men were now on her side too and beginning to make their way up behind her. She waited for them and when Alex reached the top he walked over and hugged her tightly.

'Thanks, Rose. You saved my ass.'

She hugged him back and nodded.

Jacob took the lead again with Alex bringing up the rear as they rejoined the path they had lost and continued up towards the shrouded peak. Whilst they had been moderately sheltered in the gully, the wind and the rain had picked up considerably and the thunder in the distance was much closer.

The path was more easy going now, with just a few short scrambles which were slick with rain as they made their way up and onto the flat summit. As they approached the cairn which marked the top, Rose felt disappointed, having hoped to see an inversion. She knew the chances were slim, but she had briefly imagined what a special sight it would've been for them to experience together, with stunning views of the Matterhorn in the distance, but today it was shrouded in mist and rain and they could barely see more than ten foot in any direction.

About a hundred metres down the path that would lead them into the valley below was a sheltered dip which Alex settled down inside. As he waited for the other two to join him, he produced a small burner and three mugs and began to make a brew.

'I'm not liking the sound of that storm,' said Jacob as he sat down on a small fold out mat. 'I think we need to move on soon, its getting closer.'

Rose loosened her hood slightly and leaned forward.

'I agree, we're too high up,' she said. 'I've been in this situation a few times. You don't fuck with lightning.'

'You were a badass back there, Rose,' said Alex, stirring the coffee with a spork he had produced from the top of his pack. 'How's your arm?'

Rose rubbed it gently.

'It'll be fine,' she said, smiling. In truth it hurt like hell, and she wondered if she might have a bruise shaped like a hand by the morning.

'I'm sorry,' said Alex, he was about to say something else when another flash interrupted him and a few moments later, the sound of thunder came tumbling overhead.

'We got time to finish our coffee?' said Alex, looking up as the rain got harder.

Jacob shrugged.

There was another flash of light and Rose counted in her head, reaching two before the rumble crashed over them.

'I'm guessing not,' he said. He turned off the burner and threw the mugs back into this rucksack as the others stood up.

Rose stood and turned back to look over towards the peak, and as she did she was blinded and deafened by a flash of lighting which lanced out of the sky and crashed into the ground, striking the cairn which minutes ago they had stood next to.

She screamed and covered her ears.

'We need to go now,' said Alex, staggering up and beckoning for her to follow, pulling Rose back by her arms and pushing her ahead of him.

'Down this way, move. Stay low.'

As Rose's vision returned, she saw the path that Alex was ushering her towards, but she realised too late that it was practically vertical, and as soon as she reached the edge she began to slip and sat down hard.

Alex gripped her hand and held it tight, then Jacob was sliding down next to her, feet first and gathering speed, aiming for a large rock just ahead to slow his descent.

There was another flash and a moment later a thunderous clap. It was further away but still too close for comfort.

'We need to find somewhere to shelter *now*,' said Jacob.

'Look for a cave or an outcrop we could get under.'

Rose was still sliding from rock to rock, her bottom bruised, scraped and battered.

Alex reached out and pulled her towards him as she stepped down from a high ledge, then he picked her up by the waist and passed her to Jacob, who lowered her down further still.

She felt like a pinball, being bounced and pushed and handled by the two men as they helped her and each other down and away from the storm. She was their precious cargo and they were keeping her safe.

As she grabbed hold of a sharp handhold, something caught her eye about thirty feet below her. She called out to the two men above, but her shout was drowned out by another blinding white flash. She didn't really hear the thunder this time, but her ears were ringing so she knew it must have been close.

She felt disoriented and dizzy and a little sick and her movements were slow and confusing. She looked up to find Jacob and Alex staring down at her, also disoriented. She shouted out again, but couldn't hear her own voice.

'Cave,' was all she managed.

Alex nodded and slid down past her, forging ahead and finding a path. As he approached the entrance he stopped and waited, beckoning to them.

Jacob yelled at him to get inside but his shout was lost by another crash of white hot light and sound.

Rose stumbled and slipped and Alex caught her and then he was bundling her inside, followed by Jacob.

*

The little cave was shallow and low, but there was just about enough room for all three of them to shelter inside. The entrance was raised too, which gave them a little extra protection from the howling wind and the driving rain.

'Are you okay?' said Jacob as they crawled inside, Rose sat down at the far end and unclipped her rucksack, rolling it off and onto the damp floor next to her. She nodded but didn't say anything.

Jacob turned as Alex crawled further inside, reaching out his hands for his friend to pull him in.

The noise of the wind was muffled in here and they could talk more easily, but for the moment they were quiet.

Light filled the cave and another thunderous clap of lightning struck nearby making Rose jump.

'Fuck me,' said Alex. 'This was not on the forecast.'

Another flash and another crash and the cave felt like it shook.

'That was bloody close,' said Jacob, peering out of the entrance.

Rose closed her eyes and breathed deeply, trying to calm herself down.

She felt someone's hand on her leg and reached out for it, finding it and gripping it tight. She didn't care if it was Jacob or Alex, she was just grateful for the comfort.

'Come out to Switzerland, we'll go camping, reconnect,' she said, half chuckling and half shaking, her eyes still closed. She coughed and held her hand over her mouth, bending forward. 'You didn't mention the *nearly dying in an electrical storm* bit.'

'Thought it might put you off, not the sort of thing you put in the brochure,' said Alex. 'Besides we'd be down in the forest now if we'd stuck with my plan.'

'Don't blame me, you said yourself the forecast didn't predict this, and if we were down in the forest it might be worse.'

'Sorry,' said Alex. 'Just blowing off steam.'

Rose glowered. 'This isn't my fault. It's no one's fault. I saved you, or have you forgotten that already?'

'We're safe now,' said Jacob, always the diplomat.

Rose stayed silent, she knew Jacob was right, but she was angry at Alex.

The cave was dark and damp and as Rose listened carefully she could hear running water.

'How long do you think we'll be in here for?' she said.

'I'm not a meteorologist, but I reckon it will pass in the next hour.'

Rose pulled her hood off and shook her hair out, sighing deeply.

She felt like that last strike had hit her. She knew it hadn't, but it had been close. Just beforehand she'd felt her skin tingling and her hair rising as the static built. She'd heard about climbers who'd been killed by lightning, laughing and photographing each other as their hair stood on end, shortly before the bolt struck. The photographs were harrowing.

Alex was unpacking his burner again and she started to relax. They were all tense, they'd been through a life threatening event and they'd come out the other side safe, that's what she had to remember. She rubbed her face in her hands and smiled as a memory popped into her head.

'Do you guys remember being out by the river in the field near Mrs Soubrey's house when that storm started?' she said.

'When we were building that dam?' said Alex.

'The one that flooded half of her field?' said Jacob, laughing.

'That's the one. I'll never forget that first lightning strike, I clung to you so hard I think I damn near broke your arm,' she said to Jacob.

He laughed. 'You were pretty scared.'

'I wasn't scared, I was with you guys,' she said as another

crash of thunder reverberated through the cave. 'You always looked after me, even now.'

'I remember you held my hand all the way back to your house,' said Jacob, smiling.

'You remember that?' she said.

Jacob nodded, slowly.

'First time a girl ever held my hand for longer than a few seconds,' he said. 'You don't forget something like that.'

'But it was me though?' she said, screwing up her face. This was new to her.

Jacob shrugged. 'You're a girl?'

'You guys never fancied me.' It was more of a question than a statement, at least she hoped it came across that way. She felt a familiar feeling of anxiety in her stomach as she waited for them to respond. The silence kept going.

Jacob looked at Alex then down at the floor.

Rose tilted her head.

'You did?' she said.

The cave flashed bright white. They waited for the rumble, looking over at the mouth, and it came a few seconds later.

'It's passing over us,' said Alex, as it faded. 'That was further away.'

Rose wasn't going to let her question go.

'Don't change the subject. Life threatening lightning storm aside. You liked me? When?'

'Does it matter?' said Jacob.

'Yes it matters,' said Rose.

'Why?'

Rose didn't answer straight away. She wasn't sure how to. She couldn't tell them she liked them. It would be too weird right now, and she couldn't pretend she only liked *one* of them either. It wouldn't be truthful and it wouldn't be fair. She was shocked too. Some part of her had always known that her feelings weren't entirely unrequited, but to hear it out loud, here and now, was a surprise.

'It doesn't matter,' she said, quietly. 'I just want to know.'

Jacob looked down, hiding his face.

Alex smiled. 'Last year of school,' he said. 'I had a huge crush on you.'

'What?' said Rose, turning to face him. 'I was asking Jacob. And no you fucking didn't, you fancied Philly West.'

'No, I *told* you I liked her because you kept on asking me who *I* liked. You kept saying that you would be my wing-girl.'

'I was asking you because I liked you, you muppet,' she said laughing. 'I wanted you to say *me*.'

She suddenly felt extremely guilty, she'd let slip that she had liked Alex, in front of Jacob. Alex shook his head and winked. 'And Jacob? When did you like Rose, eh?'

'It doesn't matter,' he said.

'Come on, please,' said Rose. 'I want to know.'

But Jacob looked awkward and upset and Rose frowned.

'What's wrong?' she said, laughing nervously.

'Nothing,' he said, he shifted uncomfortably and turned away.

Alex leaned forward. 'He's too embarrassed to tell you,' he whispered.

'What do you mean?'

Rose's eyes became wild with curiosity.

'*Alex*,' snapped Jacob, but his friend leaned closer to Rose.

'That he liked you all the way through school, and sixth form,' said Alex.

Rose didn't reply, instead she just looked at Jacob, who looked away again.

'Is that true?' she said.

After a moment, Jacob nodded.

'I'm sorry,' she said, quietly. 'I didn't know.'

'Listen,' said Alex, now feeling a little awkward. 'Storm's

gone, I think.'

In the distance there was another rumble but it sounded far away.

'I'll go take a look,' said Jacob, crawling back towards the entrance.

Rose stayed back and put her arm on Alex's shoulder. 'Is that true?'

Alex nodded. 'He crushed on you pretty hard, broke his heart when you left for Wales.'

Rose looked down, frowning. She hadn't expected this. Jacob was always shy, but over the years his behaviour towards her had changed. To begin with he'd been a friend to play with in the playground, to run around and be boisterous with, like Alex. But over time he'd become more gentleman like. He'd treated her more and more like a girl, instead of one of the boys. She didn't consider it at the time, as anything other than his personality changing. But now she understood that he had started to see her differently. Alex had too, but he'd hid it better. Perhaps for her sake, but more likely for Jacob's.

'You're a good friend to him, Alex.'

She squeezed his arm and looked up at him smiling and for a brief moment she saw a look of passion in his eyes.

Jacob called from outside. 'We're in the clear I think.'

Alex turned toward the entrance and then looked back and extended his arm to her, pulling her up into a crouch. She followed him out and stood up straight.

Jacob was standing looking at a rock about fifteen feet above and away from them.

'Come and look at this,' he said, beckoning them over and pointing.

As Rose drew near she realised that she had been standing just a few metres from this spot, below the rock, when the lightning had struck.

What Jacob was pointing at was a large burnt crack that had now appeared in the structure of the rock, like a fissure opening in the ground. She reached out to touch it, running her fingers along the edge of the charred and melted stone. It was chilling.

'Come on,' said Alex. 'Let's keep going.'

Over the next hour they walked in silence, or near enough. The storm had shaken them, but Rose had been shaken emotionally by what she'd found out in the cave. She kept turning it all over in her mind. Not knowing how to piece it together, remembering moments from their childhood and playing them back in new ways, knowing now what she didn't understand back then.

Both of them had liked her.

In some way she had always known it. It was as though she had been unable to process it or see it before. As though her mind had decided that it was impossible, and had just sought out the negatives, the things that confirmed her belief that they would never feel the same way, and had filtered out the positives, along with any evidence that they did.

An hour later, as they arrived at their new camp, she found herself preoccupied with her thoughts and she drifted around helping the two men as they setup their home for the night, put up their tent (just the one tonight she noted with excitement), and built another fire pit for later, but she couldn't stop thinking.

She hadn't been honest with them, and they hadn't been honest with her.

Now they *had* been honest with her, but *she* hadn't told them the truth.

That she loved them.

But she was going to. Somehow.

She must do it. But did she have the courage?

Either way, it was exciting.

Her feelings weren't unrequited, and they never had been.

*

It was late, but Rose wasn't tired. She was much too excited to sleep and the heat was making her feel uncomfortable. The storm had created a layer of humidity and the night seemed to be warming up, not cooling down.

Alex was still outside, and she listened to him as he moved around making sure everything was away and safe.

Jacob had unzipped his sleeping bag and was dozing beside her, wearing nothing but a tight fitting pair of black boxers. Rose was finding them very distracting.

She was still finding it hard to process what they had both told her in the cave. Had she really been that oblivious? She now knew that they had liked her, at different times, and she was finding it so frustrating that they hadn't acted upon it, and that she hadn't either. But she'd assumed that they'd had brief and confused crushes.

She started to think about all those missed opportunities, afternoons spent lazing around in the woods with one of them or the other. Hours spent watching TV or playing games, huddled next to one of them or laying between them (she grinned as she thought about that). All it might have taken was a squeeze of a hand, a touch of skin, and then a kiss.

She wished she could go back.

It was getting hot and the thoughts running through her mind weren't helping. She undid her sleeping bag, laying it out flat and then shimmied out of her leggings. The cool air on her bare skin felt good. She was so glad she'd shaved her legs.

She wasn't wearing the most attractive underwear. They

weren't high waisted granny pants, but the idea of sleeping in this heat in anything but her knickers was nauseating. Next she unclipped her bra and removed it from underneath her loose white top, tucking it under Alex's makeshift jumper pillow.

Now she felt comfortable, but she was still buzzing. Her mind was going round and round in circles. Remembering times with them where something could have happened, but it didn't. So many missed opportunities.

Alex had liked her. Jacob had liked her.

And she had run away, oblivious.

She wasn't going to let it happen again. If there was any chance that this trip was rekindling any feelings the two of them might have had for her, then she was going to act on it. She wasn't going home with regrets. Not this time.

She wanted to touch herself again. She wanted to touch them. She wanted them to touch her.

She wanted them inside her.

The noise of the tent opening startled her out of her thoughts but she relaxed as she saw Alex's face appear at the entrance. He smiled as he crawled in, raising his eyebrows as he saw her long and naked legs. She screwed up her nose at him in a mock sneer and then smiled.

'I'm going to leave the door open and close the flysheet,' he whispered. 'Much too hot in here.' He glanced down at her legs again as he spoke.

She moved them aside so he had space to sit down and turn around as he zipped up the mesh inner. Then he was stripping off his shirt and throwing it into the corner. Rose couldn't help but stare as he winked back.

He crawled up past her and gripped her thigh for a fleeting moment, squeezing it before rolling onto his side on top of his own sleeping bag.

'You're so cheeky,' she said, giggling quietly.

He lay back, looking up at the roof of the tent as Rose lay back down, turning on her side to face him and tucking her hands under her cheek.

'So you did like me?' she said. 'All those years ago.'

Alex looked thoughtful for a moment before nodding. He pulled his knees up to his chest suddenly, then unbuckled his belt and removed his trousers, sliding them off awkwardly but efficiently inside the small space of the tent.

Rose tried but couldn't resist glancing down.

'Eyes up here, Prim,' laughed Alex. 'Besides you haven't evened the score yet.'

Rose grinned mischievously.

As he turned back to face her, she grabbed the hemline of her top and pulled it up and over her face, revealing her breasts just for a second.

The rush of exhilaration was dizzying.

When she covered herself up again, she found Alex with his eyes wide and his mouth open and she tried hard not to laugh.

'There, now the score is even. Well, sort of, I haven't seen anything,' she said, glancing down again at Alex's crotch. 'Doesn't seem fair to me.'

As she peeked, she thought she saw movement down there. Was he getting hard? She could see that his mind was racing.

She looked into his eyes and found they were burning so brightly with lust that it scared her a little. She could tell he wanted to lean across and kiss her, but he wasn't going to. Not with Jacob behind her. The conflict in his face was like a raging battle.

Time to take a risk.

She reached down and brushed her hand across his chest, holding her palm against it for a moment. Then she slid it down between his pecks and across his stomach.

For a while she stayed there, stroking his abs and tracing her fingers over the bumps and crevices, eager to go on, but taking it slow.

They were at the precipice. If she continued, they would go over the edge and everything would be different. The meaning of the last ten years would change and it could never go back. She still had time to stop, to change her mind and pretend she was just teasing, like two teenagers pushing the boundaries of the other to see which one breaks first.

She made up her mind.

Smiling, she raised a finger to her lips as she flattened the palm of her hand and slipped it inside his underwear, searching and feeling and then closing her fingers around his cock and as soon as she did, it felt like fireworks were exploding inside her head.

It was actually happening.

They weren't going to make love, not without waking Jacob and she wasn't sure if she was ready for that yet anyway, but *something* was happening.

For years she had wanted them, and over the last two days things had changed. Maybe it was being away for three years, or maybe it was all of them being a few years older and little more mature. Either way, this wouldn't have happened back then, it couldn't have. They were too young, too fickle and immature. But now it was, and it felt right. It felt good. It felt incredible.

She slid her hand up and then down his shaft slowly.

Really slowly.

She wanted to savour it, not rush it.

To feel every twitch and pulse.

To see every expression of pleasure.

Rose could feel him harden in her grip, she wanted him inside her so much, but not with Jacob asleep next to them.

One step at a time.

She loosened her fingers and played with his head, running her thumb over the tip and down and around, and she watched eagerly as he strained and writhed to her touch as the fingers he'd once dreamt of simply holding in his hand, pleasured him.

Now she ran those fingers lightly down his shaft and underneath, feeling for his balls and finding them. She cupped them in her grasp and rolled them back and forth, and then she was clasping his thick member in her palm again firmly and thrusting her hand up and down.

It felt surreal.

She half wondered if she was dreaming.

For ten years she had wanted this moment, and for so many countless lonely nights she had dreamt of it. Now it was actually happening.

Well, almost.

Alex closed his eyes, unable to focus now, feeling Rose's soft and supple hands sliding up and down him and then he felt himself pulse deep inside.

He was going to orgasm, she could sense it. He wasn't going to last. He couldn't, even if he tried. She understood, and it made her feel so incredibly happy and special.

His mouth was open, his eyes were beginning to glaze over and lose focus and his whole body was stiffening and twitching.

She suddenly realised he was going to cum on the groundsheet, and she didn't want that. She didn't want him to waste his seed by letting it spray over the canvas, so impulsively, she wriggled closer to him.

With her free hand she pulled on the elastic of her knickers and slipped the head of his cock inside, pressing his wet glans up against her opening and holding the material of her underwear against his shaft.

He sensed what she was doing and she felt him surge and

thrust and convulse in silence and then his arm shot out and held onto her naked hip to steady himself as he came against her.

Alex was cumming by her touch.

Her Alex.

Hers at last.

She could feel his warmth spreading inside her knickers, rope after rope of cum splashing against her lips and pooling around and against her, sticky and wet.

As he kept on twitching and squeezing she felt an unexpected climax building within herself, and to stop from crying out she shot forward and kissed him hard on the lips.

For just a second the head of his still hard cock slipped inside her pussy and then out again, and she came.

Alex's strong arms held her tightly as she shook, her mouth wide open, their foreheads pressed together, his other arm now holding her cheek as she shuddered and tried to control her breathing.

For one brief, heavenly second, Alex had been inside her.

Other men had fucked her and made love to her, but none of them had made her orgasm. She'd always just pretended, gone through the motions and told them it was great. Alex had accidentally slipped inside her for a second and she had climaxed.

Her body was still quivering, but her breathing was slowing down now. She looked up into his eyes again and then kissed him, long and hard.

It felt like they were making up for lost time. His lips pushing urgently against hers, her tongue searching and pressing into his mouth. Both of them were doing their best to be quiet and to not wake up Jacob, but both were finding it hard to restrain themselves. After a while they stopped and lay next to each other, looking into one another's eyes, unable to speak and trying to say everything with their expressions.

Eventually, Alex fell asleep, unable to keep his eyes open any longer. His body finally, yet unexpectedly satisfied and spent, he dropped into a deep slumber.

But Rose was still wide awake. She was still struggling to take in what had just happened. This was what she had always wanted, but not just Alex, she wanted Jacob too.

She wanted more.

She'd had a taste now. Not literally, but hopefully that would come.

She wanted them both.

Feeling naughty again, she slipped her fingers inside her underwear and found the sticky warm spot where Alex had cum, sliding up and down and playing with it as she thought about his face in the moment he'd climaxed.

She wanted to see Jacob's face too.

She was getting aroused again.

Jacob was snoring quietly and he shifted beside her.

Rose rolled over to look at him.

He opened his eyes and looked around and then saw that she was awake.

'Can't sleep?' he whispered.

Rose shook her head.

'Another bad dream?' he mouthed.

She shook her head again and reached out for his hand.

She entwined her fingers in his and stroked his knuckle with her thumb, then brought him close to her lips and kissed the back of his wrist. She breathed in deeply, her eyes closed and when she opened them she found Jacob staring wild and confused, but that look was back. That way that he had looked at her as they'd wrestled in the dirt the day before. As he'd pinned her down with his strength and body.

He was more hesitant than Alex though.

Shuffling forward, she reached up with her hand and placed it on the side of his face, looking deep into his eyes and glancing down at his lips.

Jacob's nerves betrayed his eyes. She could feel his hand shaking in hers and she loved him all the more for it. She could tell he wanted to kiss her, so she leaned forward and softly and quietly, pressed her lips against his and waited for him to kiss her back.

It didn't take long.

As soon as her lips touched his, Jacob's hands slid up her side and pulled her close to him with a strength that surprised her and in response she wrapped her arm over his back, feeling his muscles ripple as he pressed himself against her body.

Only minutes ago Alex had cum inside her knickers and then made her orgasm with just the tip of his cock, and now Jacob was kissing her with such passion and energy that she thought she might climax again from just the touch of his lips.

Her mind was racing. Every fibre of her being wanted this, but she knew what was happening was wrong. She was committing a betrayal of trust. It wasn't cheating in the strictest sense of the word, but in a way, cheating is exactly what this was. But how could she resist when she knew how much they both wanted her? She had spent years wanting them, sometimes Alex more than Jacob, sometimes Jacob more than Alex, but it didn't matter in the end. She knew now that she had always loved them both, and always would. She wanted this, and they wanted her. After years of sexual tension, teasing, repression and angst, she couldn't hold back the dam any longer.

She felt Jacob's erection pressing against her crotch, and she parted her thigh just enough to let him know that it was okay. Then she reached down.

He jumped as Rose's fingers closed around him, instinctively grabbing for her hand, but then stopping himself. He found her smiling back at him, eyes wide in the darkness, glowing, almost pleading. Rose searched again and found him, closing her fingers back around his shaft and started sliding them up and down slowly.

Jacob was slightly larger than Alex, which surprised her. She had always assumed that Mr Cocksure would have the bigger cock, but she was happy to be wrong. He also seemed a little more reticent, less lustful and more, something else. She wasn't sure what.

She saw him look over at his sleeping friend and then back at Rose questioningly, who shrugged and smiled and stared into his eyes with lust as she began to speed up.

Her fingers touched his face as she kept going, her thumb running down his cheek and finding the corner of his lip, as she caressed him.

Now Jacob was getting close too. She could sense the subtle differences between them. Alex had tensed up to the point where it felt like his muscles would burst, but Jacob was more relaxed, more in control. His breathing was more regulated. He was more passionate and less urgent. She could tell he wanted this to last.

But Rose wanted it *right now* she needed it.

She looked into his eyes and smiled as she slid smoothly across the canvas towards him and then just as before, with Alex's seed still warm between her thighs, she pulled her underwear out and positioned him, pressing him up against her, this time sliding him up and down the length of her lips and then swirling him over her clit as she pleasured him slowly and carefully.

She could feel him building up now too, and again it was different to Alex, his orgasm was deeper, more profound and with more feeling.

He loved her.

As she realised this, she nearly stopped stroking him.

He wasn't reluctant because he was concerned about his

friend, although she knew that would be a part of it, nor was it that he was being too polite.

This just wasn't how he had wanted it to happen. He wanted to make love to her.

She understood all of this in a matter of seconds and she suddenly felt tremendous guilt.

Jacob loved her and she loved him, and maybe Alex did too.

He twitched firmly in her palm and she gripped him tightly and then, without a second thought, she guided him to her lips and slipped him inside.

This is what he wanted.

She felt it straight away. He surged inside her, stretching her and making her feel whole.

As his body became one with hers, she kissed him and looped both arms around his neck as he thrust into her.

Once.

Twice.

Then she felt it again, the warmth spreading inside her.

Jacob's warmth.

She felt him shuddering and erupting and within seconds she came too, squeezing him as she tightened and contracted over and over.

Just like Alex, she had come almost straight away, the moment his cock had entered her body. It was like she was made for them, and she had waited so long, too long for their touch, so that when she felt them inside her, her body just couldn't contain itself.

She took his hand in hers again, kissing it as quietly as she could and then he was holding her face and kissing her lips over and over, whilst squeezing her tight in his arms.

As Jacob relaxed and started to drift off to sleep, she became aware of Alex behind her again, snoring quietly.

She was also aware that her pussy was warm, satisfied and

gloriously wet.

As the afterglow faded, reality began to set in and so did her anxiety. She had let both of them fuck her. One after the other, without each others knowledge, inside the same tent.

Shit, she thought.

This is going to get complicated in the morning.

*

CHAPTER FIVE

Rose had barely slept.

All throughout the night her mind had been racing. What should she say to them both? What *could* she say?

She *had* to say something. To both of them. Because it wasn't going to take forever for them to figure out something was up.

She didn't want to regret last night, but it was a mistake. One that she was likely to pay for with the loss of their friendship and she couldn't bare the thought of that. It was tearing her apart.

It might even tear them apart.

She felt terrible.

In the heat of the moment, she had been unable to control herself. Years of lust, desire and repression had caught up with her, like a dam bursting. It had felt so good. Both of them had made her orgasm harder than she ever had before, and she had made them both cum. But now she was lying next to them, she was finding it hard to rationalise what had happened.

What was she going to say to them?

She had to be honest.

There was no other way forward.

She lay awake staring at the canopy of the tent, feeling as though she was waiting for her own execution.

Alex was the first to stir. He rubbed his eyes and yawned and then turned his head to look over at her with a smile so wide and so full of joy that it broke her heart.

She tried to hide the pain as she smiled back, but it was hard and Alex knew something was up.

'What's wrong?' he mouthed at her.

Rose still didn't know what to say, so she just shook her head but her eyes were brimming with tears.

'It's okay,' said Alex, reaching out to touch her face and comfort her, but she pushed his hand away. He frowned and looked hurt.

'Did I do something wrong?' he asked more loudly, he looked panicked now.

She shook her head from side to side viciously. 'No,' she said and squeezed his fingers as she lay them back by his side.

She could feel Jacob rolling over now beside her and as he did, Alex's expression changed, and then strangely it became a grin. He was looking down toward's Jacob's crotch.

Rose turned over in horror and followed his gaze to find that Jacob's cock was still outside of his boxers, and he had a hard on.

She froze, waiting for Alex to say something, but instead he laughed.

'Morning sunshine,' he said loudly. 'Feeling glorious?'

'Huh?' said Jacob frowning.

Rose looked away as Jacob caught up.

'Oh shit,' he said, as he tucked himself back in. 'Sorry.'

He rolled the open edge of his sleeping bag over himself.

'Nice dream?' said Alex, still laughing.

'Something like that,' moaned Jacob, still groggy.

Rose blushed a little as her stomach cramped. She watched as he stretched and sat upright, rubbing his eyes.

She was on edge. She had to be honest with them. It was the right thing to do. There was no other way to deal with this, other than the truth and it had to be soon.

'I think we made a deal about breakfast?' said Alex, yawning again. 'Might be able to cook outside this morning. Sounds like the weather's moved on.'

'Last full day,' said Jacob, stretching forward and unzipping the tent as Alex shifted forward.

Beautiful sunshine shone through the gap and the fresh dew on the grass felt refreshing as the damp air drifted in through the opening.

Alex stepped out onto the grass and Rose watched him stretch, his muscles rippling and extending. She turned to look at Jacob and found him smiling at her, he peeked outside and then leant in for a cheeky kiss but Rose pulled away, shaking her head.

Jacob frowned and she could see he was hurt too, and her heart cracked a little more. Any more of this and it would break in two.

'What's wrong?' asked Jacob quietly.

'What are you two whispering about?' said Alex, reappearing at the entrance, frowning.

Rose looked from one to the other, so many thoughts running through her head, and then she said, 'I can't do this.'

She got up and pushed her way out of the tent, tears streaming down her face and started to walk away.

Jacob came out of the tent after her and Alex stood up, confused and concerned.

'Rose, what's wrong?' said Jacob.

'Where are you going?' said Alex.

She turned around, vulnerable and tearful, wearing just her knickers and her loose white top, her thighs bruised from the climbing, her arm bruised from Alex. Her eyes streaming with tears.

'I love you both,' she said.

The two men looked at each other, and then back at her.

'There, I said it. I've been wanting to say it for ten fucking years,' she said, through heaving sobs. 'I love you both.'

Then she turned around and walked away.

*

'Rose, come back,' said Jacob, calling after her and chasing her down the slope. He had shoes on and she didn't, so he was gaining on her quickly.

Rose's feet were in pain. She had already cut her sole twice and was bleeding freely as snot was dripping down her face. She didn't know where she was going. There was no plan, she just knew she had to get away from them, not for her sake but for theirs.

'Just leave me alone,' she shouted back at him. 'I don't need you to fucking rescue me.'

'Stop,' he shouted. 'You're going to hurt yourself.'

As he spoke she slipped, but managed to stay upright, still moving, but Jacob was going to catch up with her.

'Where are you going?' he said, as she felt his hand on her shoulder. She shrugged him off but lost her balance and he caught her as she fell.

'Stop touching me,' she shouted. 'Fucking hell, Jacob you've always got to be the fucking hero don't you? Always trying to fix me or save me, or keep me safe.'

'What are you talking about?' he said, helping her to stand

up.

Alex was coming down the hill now too.

'What the fuck is going on?' he said as he approached, sliding down the shale toward them.

'Last night,' said Rose.

Both of the men's expressions froze.

'You both know what I'm talking about,' said Rose, still crying.

There was a long silence. Rose didn't have to say anything more.

Jacob frowned. 'Both of us?' he said and turned to look at Alex. The two men stared at each other, open mouthed and then turned back to Rose.

'Are you fucking kidding me? Him too?' said Alex.

Rose nodded.

Jacob took a step back, frowning.

'I love you both,' said Rose, her shoulders sagged. Now the truth was out there, all of her energy seemed to fade away.

She sat down on the floor and sobbed.

'What the fuck, Rose?' said Alex. 'So you finished me off and then rolled over and jacked him too? Or was it the other way round? Which one of us got sloppy seconds, eh?'

'Does it matter?' said Jacob.

'Yes it fucking matters,' said Alex and he pushed Jacob away. His friend stumbled backwards and tripped on a rock, landing hard on the ground beyond.

Within a second he was up, and running towards Alex.

Rose screamed as they collided, a cloud of dust rising from where the pair of them fell.

Alex's fist found its way into Jacob's stomach and then Jacob kneed Alex in the thigh, each man an equal match for the other, both trying to land blows.

'You fucking prick,' shouted Alex, swinging his elbow toward Jacob's chin. 'Get the fuck off me.' He connected and

Jacob grunted and rolled onto the grass of the hillside and kept on going to create some distance before he got back up.

Rose ran between the two of them and screamed again, holding up her hands.

'Stop,' she shouted. 'Stop fighting. This isn't your fault.'

Alex was still moving towards Jacob, his eyes filled with rage. Jacob was looking at Rose though.

'Listen to her, Alex. This is pointless.'

'Feel's fucking good though,' he snarled, still stalking forward.

Rose stepped into his path and grabbed both of his arms and he stopped.

'I love you,' she said, catching his eyes. 'I always have.'

'What about him then?' he pointed.

'I love him too. It's why I left, because I was afraid that neither of you would ever love me back.'

'You can't love us both,' said Alex. 'That's bullshit.'

'I do,' said Rose, doing her best to calm him down. 'In different ways and you know I do.'

Alex turned his attention on Jacob again.

'Did it feel good after all these years, mate?' he said, still belligerent. 'Finally getting your end away?'

'Stop, please,' said Rose. 'I never wanted this.'

'Not sure what you were expecting,' said Alex.

Jacob was looking from her to Alex and then back to her, his face a mixture of anger and resignation, but then all of a sudden, he turned around and walked away, trudging back up the hill towards the camp.

Alex's shoulder's relaxed and he took a few steps back and sat down on a nearby rock.

After a moment he started to laugh.

Rose just stared at him.

About halfway up the hill, Jacob turned around and stood still.

'You two coming?' he said, rubbing his chin where Alex's elbow had caught him.

Alex was still laughing, but he stood up and whilst shaking his head he started up towards the camp following Jacob.

'Come on, Rose,' said Alex. 'Time to get dressed.'

Rose stood still for a while longer, watching the two of them walking away back up the hill.

She didn't understand what had just happened, but she was cold and had started to shiver. She nodded, then wiped her eyes and followed.

At the camp, Jacob was boiling some water and had set out three mugs filled with instant coffee.

Alex walked over and sat down on the log opposite and looked out across the landscape, letting out a long sigh.

As Rose limped back into the camp, she walked past them both to their shared tent.

She'd never even erected her own last night and now she dearly wished she had. Right now she wanted her own space, somewhere she could hide and not have to face them.

Instead she was looking for her jumper in the same spot that everything had happened in last night. She couldn't find it, so instead she put on Alex's.

It was poetic and she hated it.

A few minutes later she returned and sat down opposite them. Jacob nodded to the cup of steaming coffee on the floor in front of her. She picked it up and held it between the palms of her hand.

'Thank you,' she said, quietly.

For some time they all sat in silence. Alex's anger gradually subsiding, Rose's tears drying up and Jacob's rational side returning. The fight had changed something, but she wasn't sure what yet.

She realised after a while that they were waiting for her to speak.

'I'm sorry,' she said.

Alex nodded and Jacob sipped at his coffee, half looking at her, half trying to avoid her eye.

'I love you too,' he said suddenly. Alex didn't even look up. 'I always have. Ever since we met back at the start of school, I've loved you. I think Alex does too.' He looked out over the mountains behind her.

'At first it was a sort of innocent excitement over being friends with a girl I think. You were this fun, rough, bundle of energy that just wanted to run around, kick a football, climb a tree. I thought you were cool. After a while though, I started to realise that I missed you when you weren't around. I'd miss Alex, of course. He was my mate, but when you weren't there, I wanted you to be.'

Rose blushed. She hadn't been expecting this, and it was nice to hear, but as he continued, she wondered if she was going to like where he was going.

'For a long time I thought you liked Alex, and it broke my heart. He was cooler and tougher, and I just figured you were more into that. You found him funnier than me too, I think.'

Alex laughed. 'That's cos I am, mate.'

Jacob smiled and continued.

'But it didn't change how I felt about you, it just made it more painful.'

Rose listened carefully, she knew she shouldn't speak.

'When you left, my heart broke again but some small part of me knew it was for the best. You grew more distant, and I let it happen. I didn't try, because as far as I knew, you didn't love me. I didn't want to love someone who didn't love me back. I didn't have much choice though, that's the thing about falling in love. Time is a great healer, but my love for you left a scar on me.'

Alex chuckled. 'Starting to get a little pretentious, mate.'

Jacob nodded and smiled. 'It did though,' he continued. 'And the moment that Alex suggested we see if you were up for this trip, all those feelings came flooding back and clouded my judgement.'

'I'm sorry,' said Rose. 'I should never have come.'

'No, I'm glad you did.'

Alex was nodding.

'I'm telling you this now, because I think we've all been dishonest, and it's got us nowhere.'

Rose nodded too and looked down at the ground, wiping her nose with her sleeve. Her elbows resting on her knees.

'I still love you, Rose. I always will,' said Jacob. 'And I don't want this to be the end of our friendship. Any of us.'

Rose looked up again, hopeful.

'But I don't know, it's not that simple,' he said and looked away from her.

Alex sighed deeply.

'Fuck it, Jacob already said it, but he's right. I've always loved you. I think it took me longer than Mr Poetic here to figure it out, but he's not wrong. Ever since day one.'

He shook his head and started drawing a circle in the dirt with his finger.

'Ironically, I used to think you liked him more than me too, he was smarter, quicker, more chilled, less angry. I was *macho man*, and he was *settle down with three kids daddy material*. It hurt like fuck. I've not got the same way with words that my man Jacob here has, but I love you too. There's no one else like you that I've ever met that makes me feel the way you do.'

Rose smiled at him through her tears, wiping them away with her now sodden sleeve.

'I don't know what the fuck we're supposed to do now, though?' said Alex, laughing.

Rose laughed too, but Jacob didn't. He just smiled and

looked at the floor.

Rose wiped her nose again and took a deep breath.

'I'm sorry. I know I keep saying it, but I am,' she said, her voice wobbling. 'I've been selfish and stupid and last night I got carried away. I just wanted you both so much. I always have done, like you've both said, since day one. But it's not that simple.'

Alex sat upright, listening to her as she continued.

'Do you remember sixth form prom night?'

Jacob smiled and nodded.

'We all went together,' she said. 'I thought at the time, it was because you two were too afraid to ask anyone else. I didn't really get it, you were both gorgeous and smart and likeable, but you wanted to go with me. That night we all danced together and ate together and sang together, and it was perfect. That was the night I realised, and I mean really understood, that I wanted to be with both of you. I didn't want to be made to pick one, or not have either of you. I wanted you both. I wanted you both to kiss me, to hold me.'

She paused and looked down.

'To make love to me.'

Alex grinned and raised his eyebrows.

'But it was also the night I realised that could never happen. I saw all these other girls at the after party, pairing off with boys and finding quiet corners to snog and whatever else they were doing, and there was the three of us, awkwardly dancing by that stage, a little unsure of what to do, so we left and grabbed a bottle of vodka from the bar on the way out and sat in a field drinking until the sun came up.'

'Jacob threw up in Mrs Soubry's strawberry bushes,' laughed Alex.

Rose smiled and continued.

'When I got home that morning, I cried for two hours straight. Mum was about ready to call the police, she thought someone had raped me. I ended up telling her that a boy I liked had kissed a girl I hated and she left me alone for a bit.'

Jacob frowned and smiled at her, sympathetically as she went on.

'That was the night I decided I had to leave, to move away as far as I could. I couldn't take it any longer, not being able to have you both the way I wanted you. The choice became friendship or nothing, and I had to choose nothing to stop myself going crazy.'

Alex smiled kindly at her.

'Coming here, seeing you both again. It stirred up feelings I haven't had for two years. I'm not going to pretend I haven't thought about you both, a lot. Last night was the culmination of that. I couldn't help it, I've wanted you both for years and last night I had the chance and I took it and I'm sorry. I'm not even sure if it's what either of you wanted, or if you wanted more. But it happened, and I fucked up and I can't take it back and it was amazing.'

Tears brimmed in eyes again. 'I love you both and I've fucked this up so bad.'

Jacob stood up and walked over to her, then sat down and put his arm around her.

A few moments later, Alex stood up and did the same, sitting down beside her and comforting her as she cried.

As she felt both men holding her, she began to sob hard, her whole body wracked with guilt and sorrow and sadness and grief.

For a brief moment, she had got what she wanted.

She had loved them both and she had lost them.

*

Rose had got changed inside their shared tent. For a while she had sat still, staring at the canvas floor and thinking about last night.

She had ruined everything.

But then Jacob and Alex had comforted her, put their arms around her and held her as she'd cried. She didn't deserve them, and they didn't deserve her. She would drive a wedge between them and she couldn't bear the thought of them losing each other. It might already be too late.

This was something that she had to fix.

She pulled on her boots, laced them up and backed up out of her tent.

Turning around she saw that both of the men were repacking their bags.

Alex looked at her, and flashed a brief but kind smile.

'Hey,' he said. 'You almost ready?'

Rose frowned. 'No, we've got to take the tent down still.'

'Leave it,' he said. 'We've got a new plan.'

Jacob smiled at her too and said, 'You're going to need a towel though.'

Rose was utterly confused and remained still, a questioning look on her face trying to work out what was going on. An hour ago the two men were tussling in the dust, and Jacob's chin was already showing the first sign of a bruise.

Now they were smiling at her, and they had come up with some sort of new plan for the day.

'Don't just stand their gawping, we're not man-meat. Pack light, you won't need much, just a towel and maybe a change of clothes,' said Alex.

'What are we doing?' she said.

'Guess,' said Jacob.

A few minutes later, after repacking her bag, she was ready to go, she didn't have a towel but she'd stuffed a thick fleece into the top of her rucksack and left a bunch of extra bits and bobs on the canvas floor. She didn't really know what to leave without knowing exactly what the men were planning, but she had a good idea.

When she came out of the tent, the two of them were sat on a rock together laughing and waiting for her. As though nothing had happened at all.

She walked over, utterly confused and a little nervous.

'What are we doing?' she said.

'That would ruin the surprise,' said Jacob.

'Come on, Prim,' said Alex jumping down. 'Follow us.'

Jacob joined him and the two set off together in front of her. As she walked behind them, they talked animatedly to one another and Rose couldn't help but feel a little hurt that one of them wasn't behind her, keeping her safe. She suddenly felt vulnerable, but if this was to be her punishment for last night then there were worse things. She certainly deserved worse, she thought.

Or maybe that was the plan?

She stopped walking.

'I want to go home,' said Rose, but saying it out loud made the idea seem utterly foolish. What was home to her? She didn't have a home, as such. The closest thing was back with her parents.

The two men slowed down and turned around.

'You're free to,' said Alex. 'You've got a map.'

Rose stood, feeling silly.

'Where are you taking me?' she said.

'What are you afraid of?' said Jacob.

Rose shrugged, then Alex smiled.

'We don't want you to leave,' said Alex. 'Today was always going to be a surprise, there's a place near here we want to show you. Something special. If you want to come with us, great. If not, we're still going to go.'

Rose looked from Alex to Jacob and back again. It was as though all had been forgiven or forgotten. Rose realised in that moment that the two men were stronger friends than she had given them credit for. They weren't going to let her get between them. They hadn't for the last ten years and one night wasn't going to change that. That's part of what she loved about them, they were strong. They had a bond that was unbreakable. They were such different characters but they complimented each other and came out better for it.

She loved them so hard it hurt, but they loved each other too, in a different way and she wanted so much to be a part of it.

She would stay, where else would she ever want to be?

She nodded, took a deep and unsteady breath, and started walking again, catching up to them and walking beside them as they continued up the track.

Soon they arrived at the edge of a large forest that seemed to nestle and scale up the side of a vast and steep rock face.

Alex produced his GPS tracker and began to use it to find their route, pointing through dense foliage and thick clumps of trees. At times they had to clamber across roots and small rivers, helping each other as they went. Passing their bags to one another and jumping, catching and laughing. They were enjoying each other's company again, as they always did. It came so easily to them all.

It reminded Rose of all the times they had spent exploring the woods outside the old village, playing on rope swings, climbing trees, building dens.

As they kept moving, Rose became aware of a noise which sounded like television static getting closer and closer, and then all of sudden Alex stepped out into a pool of sunshine.

As she followed, Jacob now behind her, she found they had worked their way into a small lagoon, fed by the most beautiful waterfall that Rose had ever seen.

The fall itself appeared to be tunnelling straight out of the cliff face, from a cave just below a line of trees which had sprouted atop the massive overhanging bulkhead of cliff before them. A huge gouge in the face of the rock had created a natural shelter behind the water itself, and a rocky beach had formed over most likely thousands of years of erosion from the splashing water.

The lagoon itself was a mixture of turquoise and teal, darkening in shade as the pool deepened towards the centre.

But the most striking thing of all was the stunning rainbow which shimmered in the air in front of them, suspended in the fine cooling mist that hung and drifted on the wind.

It was the most beautiful sight that Rose had ever seen and she stood staring up and around in childhood wonder at the breathtaking landscape that surrounded them.

It was paradise.

Alex was the first to move, taking hold of her hand, much to her surprise, and pulling her with him along the rocks toward the small beach beneath the fall. High up, where the ground was almost level he dropped his rucksack and began to strip off.

'Come on,' he said to the others. 'Last one in buys the beers.'

Rose laughed but Jacob was already racing to undress.

She suddenly felt competitive and she pulled her fleece top up and over her head then sat down to hurriedly remove her shoes and then to her surprise and shock, she realised that Alex was stripping down completely.

He was going to skinny dip.

She stopped, her mouth wide as he whipped off his boxer shorts revealing his toned behind and then ran down to the rock suspended ten foot above the water, followed seconds later by an equally naked Jacob.

'You lose, Rose!' shouted Alex as he dived headfirst into the clear blue pool of fresh, stunning water.

She sat there as Jacob leapt in after his friend, her mouth

still open wide, her sock half way off her foot, completely frozen.

What the hell were they doing?

She didn't know what to do. Should she strip down too? Should she be a prude and just strip to her knickers and bra? Should she just stay clothed and watch, like some sort of lovelorn perv?

Alex resurfaced and swam backward slowly, looking at her.

'Oi,' he said. 'Stop gawping and get naked.'

That rather settled it then.

Not entirely reluctantly she stripped down as both men watched. As she reached her underwear she began to feel self conscious and called out to them both.

'Turn around then,' she shouted.

'Not a chance,' came the reply from Alex.

She grinned, and shook her head in mock despair.

'Fine,' she said.

She unclipped her bra and let her breasts fall loose as Alex let out a wolf whistle of approval. She sneered at him, wrinkling her nose and then turned and slipped her knickers down over her bottom as Jacob began to clap.

Now she walked towards them, swinging her hips with a little more sway than usual, until she reached the raised rock where Alex had leapt in from.

Both men were looking up at her now, with wide grins on their faces, as she peered down at them in the nude.

She took a step back, held her breath, and dived, sliding under the water with such grace and precision that Alex felt the need to applaud.

As she emerged, she ran her hand through her wet hair and smiled, wringing it out into a tight ponytail which she tied up into a rough bun as she tread gently in the water.

The two men began to swim away from her now, heading

towards the spot where the waterfall came crashing into the lagoon.

Rose dipped beneath the surface and swam after them. The cool water felt incredible against her naked skin, and the sheer electric excitement of skinny dipping with her two favourite men was making her feel giddy. It was liberating and cathartic, as though after a decade of being reserved and restrained they were discarding their armour and being open and honest with each other.

As she reached the two of them, she found Jacob treading water and smiling whilst Alex floated on his back. They were about fifteen feet from the spray of the fall, a fine mist floating gently over them and around them all.

'Thank you for this,' said Rose. 'Not just this I mean, but everything.'

'It wouldn't have been the same without you.'

'Yeah,' laughed Alex. 'I wouldn't have fucked you in a tent for starters, mate.'

Jacob laughed quietly and turned around to look up at the waterfall.

'It's beautiful isn't it?' he said.

Rose followed his gaze.

'Like something out of a movie,' said Alex.

'I am going to miss you, Rose,' said Jacob, suddenly.

Rose blushed as Jacob turned back to look at her. She realised it was the first time he'd really looked at her since last night, and now he was gazing at her with kindness and love.

Rose wanted to swim over and hug him, but she knew she couldn't.

Then she stopped herself.

For years she had thought this way, wanting something but holding herself back from having it. What was stopping her? Nothing. She had nothing to lose anymore.

She floated closer to him, until she was inches from his

chest and then reached up and put her arms around his neck, and her head on his shoulder, holding her naked body tight against his under the water.

Alex watched, smiling.

'Do I get a naked hug if I say I'm going to miss you too?'

Rose, wrapped up and soaking wet in Jacob's big arms, smiled and turned to look at him.

'Come here,' she said.

'What, and get poked by Jacob's raging boner? I'll wait,' laughed Alex, continuing to paddle in the shallow water.

Rose just smiled and beckoned him to come closer and after a little hesitation he did, grinning and then swimming forward toward them both.

As he drew near, Rose unhooked her arms from Jacob and looped them over Alex's neck and then rested her head against his chest. She sensed movement behind her and then Jacob's body pressed against her back and he wrapped his arms around them both, in a huge bear hug.

She could feel the touch of Alex's manhood on her thigh and Jacob's against her ass and without holding back, she giggled.

'What's so funny?' said Alex. 'Is Jacob's cock really tiny?'

Rose shook her head.

'I just always wanted this,' said Rose. 'To be held by you both.'

She smiled and then looked up at them in turn.

'That all?' said Alex.

'No, I wanted you to fuck me senseless too.' As she said it, she could have sworn that Jacob's cock twinged against her.

Alex pushed away, smiling and Jacob pulled back too, wading backwards in the water.

'Come on,' said Alex. 'Let's go swim through the fall.'

As Rose watched them swim away, she felt a great wave of sadness wash over her.

This was so perfect. She never wanted it to end.

But it had to end, and it wasn't going to be the fairytale she had dreamed of for so many years.

One thing she was proud of, was being honest with them at last. After so many years of holding back, she was finally being truthful.

There was a small part of her that hoped being direct might make a difference, but she knew what they were doing. They were doing what they always had, they were bringing balance back. They couldn't bear to see her sad, lonely, or upset so they were cheering her up, making her happy, forgetting about what had happened, glossing over and making her feel loved and accepted and good again. Being candid wouldn't change anything.

But she didn't deserve it, she couldn't keep letting them do this, for her own sake and theirs.

Today though, she thought.

Maybe, let's just have today.

She could give herself that. Then she would go, and leave them for good.

Move on with her life and let them move on with theirs.

One more day of this.

One more day of bliss and fantasy, and love and joy.

It couldn't hurt.

*

CHAPTER SIX

They had returned to camp as the sun was going down, damp, happy and full of laughter. As they arrived at their tent, Alex had sat down on the rocky outcrop that looked out over the mountains and forests and rivers below and Jacob had settled down on the logs that they had manoeuvred around their little fire pit.

But Rose didn't want that, she wanted them close to her tonight.

Today's taste of paradise had made her feel pure, as though the lagoon had cleansed her and helped her to forgive herself a little.

They had spent so many years together, and so much of that time had been wasted by not being upfront and honest. Rose wished she could go back and just tell them both how she'd felt. She knew in her heart there was no way they would've understood, but she wouldn't have spent so much time wondering. Perhaps telling them how she felt would've opened up a whole new host of issues which would've plagued her thoughts for these last few years. There was little point dwelling on it, but she still knew that if she had the opportunity to do it all again, she would do it differently. She would be honest and unflinching. Rejection was far better than what they'd put each other through.

She thought back to their prom night, and how she'd felt before that evening, and how she felt right now. When they'd asked her to go to prom with them, Rose had become so excited that she hadn't slept for nearly two days. The idea of being escorted by the pair of them had been exactly what she'd been hoping for, and dreaming of. In some way she knew they both liked her, but she also knew that neither one would do anything about it, but she could hope. The night they asked, she had lain awake, dreaming up all sorts of different scenarios in which the two of them would have her. One after the other in the back of the limo, both at the same time in the bedroom of someone's after party, in a field by starlight, fumbling and sweet.

Her mother had taken her dress shopping the following week and choosing the right one had felt like one of the hardest decisions she had ever had to make. Eventually she had opted for a long, figure hugging, red silk and lace dress, low cut with an open back. It was not the sort of dress that left much to the imagination.

Her father had dropped her off at Alex's house and after an emotional farewell, he had handed her over to their care.

As soon as the boys saw her, she knew she had made the right choice.

Somehow, Jacob and Alex appeared to have aged three or four years overnight. They were waiting for her, standing up straight, arms behind their backs and smiling as she climbed out of the front seat and stood up, letting her dress fall down to her ankles.

The effect was immediate and obvious.

Alex had stuttered as he'd greeted her, and Jacob had gone bright red.

That night, after the prom had finished, they had sat in a field with their bottle of vodka, close enough to touch, an electricity between the three of them that was so intense, Rose only had to think briefly about it and she would become instantly aroused.

She wanted that again.

To feel that energy and for it to be her lasting memory of the three, all together.

If it was to be her last night with them, then they would be close.

Close enough to touch.

'Come and lay down with me,' said Rose. 'Please.'

The night air was warm, despite the clear skies, and the stars were shining like a blanket of twinkling fairy lights. There was no light pollution here, just darkness and starlight.

Rose sat down on the grassy incline and lay back, gazing upwards. As her eyes adjusted she realised that she could just about make out a river of light in the sky, and she realised as it became clearer, that it was the Milky Way.

Jacob was the first to join her, always the more rational of the two. He lay beside her, not close but not far away either.

She sensed that Alex was looking over toward them. He wasn't moving, but that was okay. She didn't want to push it. If this was to be the last night she would ever see them, it wasn't worth creating more upset. She'd done enough damage already.

But to her surprise, a moment later, he came and joined them too, laying down on the opposite side from Jacob, and a little closer.

She could feel the warmth of his body radiating off of him. She wanted so desperately to be held by them both, but now she knew that could never happen. She'd been foolish to think it might.

Still…

Laying there, hands clasped together between her breasts, she began to quietly cry.

Today had been beautiful.

More beautiful and more wonderful than she could ever have hoped and it was a perfect and fitting end to their friendship.

Something caught her eye.

She gasped as a shooting star sped across the night sky in front of them, and she pointed up.

As quickly as it appeared it was gone. She smiled as it faded away.

She made a wish.

Perhaps tonight could be the start of a wonderful new chapter in their lives? She couldn't help but feel hopeful.

She didn't know, all she knew was that she was here, now, between her two closest friends and that she felt as though she was *home*.

'This morning, all I wanted to do was go home,' she said. 'But then I realised what that feeling was, the one I felt when I read your email. You two are my home. When I read it, I knew, but I couldn't articulate it. I wanted to come home. It didn't matter where you were in the world. When we're all together, we're home. That's why I love you and I always will.'

No one spoke, none of them moved. Just the sound of the world, as it took a breath.

Alex reached across and took her hand in his, laying it down by her side and brushing her thumb with his own. The sensation sent tingles up her arm.

Then to her surprise, Jacob did the same and shifted a little closer.

They were now both near enough that she could smell their woody scent. She breathed in deeply through her nose but it was punctuated by gentle shuddering sobs.

Alex leant up next to her, looking deeply into her eyes and then he reached out with his free hand and wiped a single tear away from her cheek.

As her eyes shed another, his face came into focus and she frowned. He was looking at her differently, not with the usual cheeky mischief look.

No.

She had seen this look once before, last night.

Lust.

But this time it wasn't fading, it was burning like fire.

She suddenly found she could barely breath. She looked over at Jacob, and found him closer to her than before, and he too had that same look in his eyes.

She opened her mouth to speak but found she had no words to say, instead her whole body felt like it was filling with excitement and adrenaline, although she couldn't quite believe it. As though her skin might burst with ecstasy and delight, but she also felt exposed and vulnerable. Like the helpless prey of two ravenous predators, circling her before the kill.

She lay still, her body tingling with arousal, unsure what was about to happen.

Not knowing if she was ready for this.

Or even if *this* was *this.*

And then Alex let go of her fingers, and placed his hand flat down beside her head.

She looked nervously along the rippling muscles of his arm and back up to his face.

Then he leaned down, placed his other hand on her waist, and kissed her.

Holy shit.

This was different to last night. His kiss was long, slow and tender, but with a little force.

His lips were both soft and rough in places, and she swept her tongue across them as her hand found his arm.

Then there was another sensation, one so intense, it made her writhe and squirm with pleasure and moan out loud, her inhibition lost.

Jacob was kissing her neck.

She didn't really understand how she knew it, but she could *feel* how much he loved her. It was compassionate and kind, not rough or urgent. Like his whole persona, his kiss was slow, and smooth, and incredibly intense.

Alex began to kiss her cheek, moving away from her lips. Her breath had become short and shallow, and she shook as he kissed her ear.

Her fingers curled around the back of his neck and she pulled him in closer, and arched her head back as Jacob made his way to her shoulder. Then she felt someone's fingers searching the hem of her fleece, sliding it up over her midriff. Their fingers dragging gently across her tummy and teasing her.

Suddenly Alex was taking her arms in his hands and pinning them up behind her head as he knelt beside her, looking back down to her torso and legs as Jacob rolled her jumper up, kissing her stomach through her base layer.

She couldn't believe what was happening. Was she dreaming? Was this real? Did it matter?

Alex reached down and pulled her upright by her crossed wrists, keeping them pointed at the stars as Jacob pulled her top up and over her face. As her neckline slipped over her lips, she found she was being kissed again, forcefully. She had no idea if it was Jacob or Alex, and she loved it.

Her fleece was still covering her eyes, as her arms were being restrained in the air. Her two men were holding her and kissing her and teasing her. This was the moment she had dreamed of for so many years.

She was in heaven.

Her jumper slipped off and out through her long red hair and she saw that it had been Jacob who had been kissing her and she smiled and bit her lip.

She had no time to think before she was being laid back again by Alex, and Jacob was straddling her, pinning her torso down on the soft grass of the hill. Even if she wanted to, she was going nowhere. Just like her fantasy. But there was nowhere else she ever wanted to be.

Jacob was pulling off his top, up and over his head, then he threw it aside. The skin of his toned body glistened in the starlight.

Rose tried not to squeal with delight, but failed.

She watched with excitement and trepidation as he slid down to her feet and began to unlace her boots, throwing them aside and pulling off her thick walking socks. She tried not to laugh at how absurd it seemed, how unsexy. She wished, for a fleeting moment, that she was laying in a silk bed, dressed in lingerie but truly, she didn't care, it was funny in it's own way and that's what made it even better.

With her feet bare, he caressed them, squeezing them and running his thumb down to the sole of each one, sending waves of pleasure up through her. She closed her eyes and then opened them again as Alex leant down to kiss her once more, pinning her arms back above her head.

His free arm brushed across her breast as he reached down to undo her belt and buckle. She was powerless to resist, and loving every second.

He squeezed the clip and it popped open and then his fingers were running along the edge of her trousers, teasing her and pressing against her stomach. She writhed and squirmed at his touch, eager for him to slip his hand inside.

He let go of her arms, and she ran them through her own hair.

Then Jacob was tugging at her trouser legs and pulling them free and down, wriggling and sliding them away from her legs, exposing her knickers which were soaking wet with anticipation.

She bit her lip and let out a moan as Alex's hand rested against her pubic mound, at the same time as Jacob's hands slid up her legs, past the back of her knees and up the outside of her thighs.

Her hand reached out and gripped hold of a tuft of grass as tight as she could as her body quivered and rose and flopped back down, desperate for them to make love to her.

She wanted them to fuck her now, to throw her down and bend her over and take her one after the other, but they weren't in a rush. They were going to take their time and tease her and make this last. This was not going to be over quickly. They were savouring it.

They had wanted her for so long, they were going to have her, but at their pace. They had all the time in the world and her body was theirs to do with as they pleased, and she was giving it to them, willingly.

Jacob's hands slipped beneath the leg openings of her underwear, tracing the lining with his finger tips, up and around and back to her bottom as Alex moved down and began to kiss her stomach delicately, rolling her shirt up one caress at a time.

Jacob's lips were on her thighs now, his hands gripping her skin and he kissed her, moving higher and higher until he was an inch from her pussy.

Then he was pulling on her knickers, shimmying them down her thighs and exposing her to them both.

At the same time Alex was standing up and pulling her upright to sitting, tearing her top off over her head, leaving her in just her bra.

Both men stood back for a moment and looked at her, like two lions, their eyes prowling back and forth across her body.

She looked back at them both, feeling momentarily shy and somehow younger again. As though she was truly about to lose her virginity, vulnerable and sweet, innocent and nervous.

She bent her arms behind her back and unclipped her bra as they watched, never taking their eyes off her. She let it fall free into her hands, and then slowly uncovered her nipples.

She was naked, and entirely theirs.

Alex was the first to move, still standing up, he unbuckled his belt and let his trousers fall from his waist. Even through his underwear, Rose could see he was rock hard and huge.

It scared her a little.

She remembered how he felt in her hands last night, how she could barely wrap her fingers around him.

Now Jacob did the same, leaving his underwear in place too. Rose blushed as she remembered that Jacob was even bigger than Alex.

How was she going to do this? Could she even take them both?

They came and stood either side of her and knelt down, Alex taking her hand in his and Jacob following his lead.

As they kissed her skin and palms she slipped her hands down to their chests, running the tips of her fingers over their bodies and through their chest hair, feeling the definition of their abs.

Jacob was running his fingertips through her hair as Alex's hand ran up her stomach and brushed the underside of her breast.

She didn't know who to touch first. She didn't want to hurt one of them, to make them feel less important or desirable, but how could see choose? Although in some way, after yesterday, it might be easy.

It had to be Jacob.

She loved them both, but from what she had felt as they had briefly made love last night, it had to be him.

Her hand continued down his chest and over the edge of his underwear, feeling the shape of his bulge. Then she hooked her fingers over the elastic and pulled them down.

His cock was inches away from her lips, every millimetre of him standing to attention.

Her mouth craved him, but she took her time. She ran the tip of her finger up and down it, teasing him, looking up into his eyes and then she gripped it firmly in her palm.

Still gazing up at him, she slipped him past her lips.

He surged inside her and she heard him groan as her tongue swirled across his glans. She could feel his hands, stroking her hair softly as she took him deep into her throat and back out again.

With her other hand, she was stroking Alex's chest and now she found the edge of his underwear too, and without looking, pulled it down and began to stroke his member, sliding her palm up and down his girth as she sucked on Jacob.

She slipped him out now, licking her lips and smiling up at him and then turned to the imposing figure of Alex, his cock twitching and pulsing in her hand.

She leaned forward and teased him, instead of taking him into her mouth, she kissed him instead, working her way slowly down one side and up the other, cupping his balls with her fingers and then sliding them up the shaft as she reached the top.

Closing her eyes this time, she took him deep, as far as she could go, down into her throat, until she couldn't go any further and then back out again, swirling her tongue around him as she glided along.

She felt Jacob's hands on her back, caressing her shoulders, as she sucked his friend, quivering as he ran his fingers down her spine and through her hair.

She felt wanted and loved and safe.

Then Alex's fingers were under her chin, gently tilting her head back. She looked up at him and he smiled and gestured for her to lay back.

She did as he commanded and lay down on the grassy incline, looking up at the stars for a moment as she did. She never wanted this to end.

Jacob was in front of her, Alex to her side and she realised with a sudden panic that they were going to make love to her now. Her body was aching for them, but at the same time she was afraid. She had wanted this for so long, she didn't want to disappoint them or for anything to be wrong.

But then Alex was kneeling down beside her, and holding her hand and smiling in such a kind way that she realised that he knew, and so did Jacob. They wanted this too and they wanted it to be perfect. They were going to be kind and there was nothing that could make it wrong.

Jacob was on his hands and knees, crawling up towards her and then he stopped, spreading her legs apart as Alex squeezed her hand.

Then to her surprise, his head went down and his tongue flicked against her pussy and she cried out in pleasure.

He was going to go down on her.

As that first wave of pleasure passed, she realised that Alex's mouth had closed around her nipple and she cried out again as another wave of ecstasy spread throughout her body.

Jacob's fingers found her opening and parted her, pushing his way smoothly inside, his tongue circling her clit as Alex's tongue circled her nipple and she grabbed his head and pressed it down onto her breast. As she did her bottom rose up off the floor eager for Jacob's mouth as he tasted her.

She was going to cum, she could feel it building. The sensations were too much, overwhelming her body and she felt like she was going to explode.

'Yes,' she said, gently gripping Jacob's hair in her free hand. 'Keep going. Don't stop.'

Jacob knew what he was doing, he didn't speed up or change pace, he kept going exactly as she'd asked, her clit was throbbing with his tongue and her insides were squeezing against his fingers as she moaned and moaned and said their names over and over.

Her climax was building.

She was almost there.

Then she arched her back and went silent, her mouth wide open, squeezing Jacob's face with her thighs.

She shuddered.

Her whole body convulsed in orgasm.

Her mind went blank, as though there was nothing but her and empty space.

As she regained her senses, she felt as though her thighs were dripping and she wasn't sure if it was her, the grass or Jacob, but it felt incredible.

She was still quivering, like the aftershocks of an earthquake, little trembles shooting through her body as her fingers and toes relaxed and her thighs settled.

It had been the strongest orgasm she had ever had, and she knew it would be just the first of many tonight.

She opened her eyes and saw that Jacob was still between her legs, but he was kneeling up now. His hard cock pointed at her. He was waiting for her. Waiting for her to recover and give him permission, waiting for her to want him, to say it was okay to take her.

She nodded, and reached for him.

He crawled forward and Alex stepped back, smiling as the two of them embraced.

Jacob put his arms around her, and held her tightly, and she wrapped her arms around his back, fingers on the nape of his neck, kissing him lovingly on the lips.

He touched her cheek with the palm of his hands and looked deeply into her eyes.

'I love you,' he said.

She could feel the tip of his cock, sliding against her opening.

'I love you too,' she replied.

She opened up, and he pushed inside her.

This was it. This was the moment she had fantasised about for so many years.

Jacob was making love to her. He was inside her and he loved her, and perhaps Alex did too.

He gently began to thrust.

It felt perfect.

As Jacob continued to slip in and out of her, holding her tight in his arms beneath him, she reached out her hand for Alex's, finding it and squeezing it tightly.

Jacob was huge, each time he pushed into her it felt like she was being stretched. He wasn't as thick as Alex had felt in her palm, but he was bigger. She could feel every inch of him inside her, every vein and every bump and the shape of his head.

He started going faster, then his lips were pressing against hers again and his hand was on her breast, squeezing her. His finger tips found her nipple and pressed it and she moaned into his ear.

He leaned up and began to thrust deeper into her and then Alex was kneeling closer. She reached out and took hold of his cock.

She twisted forward and took him back into her mouth as Jacob kept thrusting.

It felt so good to have both of them inside her.

One in her mouth, the other in her pussy. It was like they were one, connected by her.

Jacob felt better than any man who had ever made love to her before. He was more pure, more manly, kinder, sweeter, more passionate, more handsome, but more importantly, more connected with her than anyone but his match, Alex. They had shared everything with her, and now they were sharing *her*.

She could feel him beginning to grow now, as though he might burst as he came, and his pace was changing and becoming more urgent. It felt incredible, and as she felt him getting closer and closer her body reacted, flushing with pleasure and making her moan and twist and then she was cumming again, like a rolling wave. She felt her pussy contracting on his cock, squeezing him, as though she was trying to milk him.

Then to her disappointment he was slowing down, and pulling back. She grabbed his legs and stopped him from pulling away, she wanted him to finish.

'Cum inside me,' she said. 'Please.'

But Jacob stopped, and she gasped as his cock slipped out of her.

'Not yet,' he said.

He was moving to lay down beside her, and then Alex was picking her up like a doll, lifting her up and onto all fours.

Jacob lay down in front of them, his cock near her mouth and then from behind her, Rose could feel Alex's hands on her ass as she realised what was happening.

She bit her lip again, and put her fingers against her pussy, feeling how wet she was after Jacob had made love to her.

Now Alex was going to fuck her.

She didn't have time to think about anything else before all of him was pushed into her, hard.

She let out a loud moan as her whole body tensed. He had

slid inside so easily, but had filled her completely. He felt different to Jacob, thicker, just as she'd thought he might be.

And harder.

Oh *fuck* he was hard.

He thrust into her, and she rocked forward.

Then he smacked her bottom and she yelped.

Again, another hard thrust.

This felt good. Really good.

She felt his hands grab her hips and then his mouth right next to her ears.

'I love you too,' he said.

She melted as she heard the words.

And then he smacked her again.

Her whole body was in ecstasy.

She looked down and saw Jacob's cock, slick with juice and slipped it into her mouth.

But as Alex began to pound her, Jacob kept slipping out and before long, it was all she could do to hold on as she got fucked mercilessly by Alex.

She was going to cum again, it felt so good from behind, different and more dirty. But Alex was different. He always had been. Jacob was the gentleman, and Alex was the animal. He was rude, he was dangerous, he was naughty and raw.

And he loved her.

His hand shifted and then she felt a single finger slide down between her cheeks. She started to panic. He was going to touch her *there*.

No one had ever done that to her before.

She had fantasised about it, but no one ha-

'Oh *fuck*, oh *shit*,' she said as his finger pressed against her sweet virgin hole, and then she was cumming.

The touch of his finger had sent her over the edge and she had cum so hard and so fast that she had screamed.

Alex kept thrusting his cock into her pussy and his finger

into her ass as she writhed and moaned and then he too pulled out of her without warning, not finishing inside her, but holding back like his friend had, and she sagged forward into Jacob's arms.

She lay there panting and sweating and quivering in his embrace as Alex rolled across and lay down. After a moment, he rolled sideways and spooned her into his big arms.

Neither of them had cum she thought. They'd held back.

They still weren't done with her.

She knew what they wanted and she wanted it to, she always had. It was her fantasy, and they wanted to fulfil it for her.

She leaned up and kissed Jacob on the lips, pulling him close to her face and then reached between his legs and found his still rock hard cock. She rolled it up and down through her palm and then pulled him towards her so he was laying on his side and facing her.

She lifted her leg so it was on top of his and angled him towards her pussy and he smiled and kissed her hard as he slipped back inside her.

Now with her free hand she searched for Alex, her hand finding his thigh and sliding around until her fingers clasped around his cock.

Then she pointed it towards her ass and pulled him towards her, urgently.

He spoke softly in her ear. 'Are you sure?'

She nodded, desperate for him.

'Fuck me in the ass,' she whispered. 'I want you both inside me.'

Alex didn't waste any time, he grabbed her cheeks and slipped his finger inside her again and she tensed and gasped, but Jacob was just beginning to find his rhythm and she didn't feel any pain, just pleasure.

Then Alex was pushing deeper into her, stretching her and

preparing her. She could feel how hard he was against her ass cheek and then suddenly he took his finger out.

Now his cock was pushing against her hole and she could feel him straining and forcing himself into her and she did her best to relax as he held her hips. She pushed backwards onto him as Jacob kept thrusting and then suddenly, he was in.

She moaned so loudly it echoed through the hills.

Jacob was inside her.

Alex was inside her.

She'd never felt so full and satisfied in all her life.

It was just as she had always imagined it.

Alex pushed again and more of his thick cock slipped into her ass, she could feel it slide up inside, like nothing she had ever felt before. It was so intense it seemed to absorb everything.

Then he stopped moving.

Jacob slowed his movements down too.

'Just relax,' said Alex, stroking her hair.

She did as he said, and immediately it felt better, more comfortable, easier and so fucking good.

Alex began to thrust, not as hard as before, but slow and short. Gentle movements.

Jacob was doing the same.

She wrapped her arm around his neck and pulled him close to her face and with her other arm she reached over her shoulder, and pulled Alex into the back of her neck.

Both of them started kissing her. Jacob on her lips and Alex on her neck and ears.

Jacob's hand was on her breast, his other arm wrapped under her. Alex's arm was tight around her hips, his other beneath her neck.

She had never felt more safe or wanted.

Jacob's cock thrust into her pussy. Alex's cock pumped into

her ass.

It was heaven.

There was something powerful building up inside of her now, something primal. She could feel that Jacob and Alex weren't going to last long either. Both of them were starting to thrust with more vigour and haste. She steadied her hand against Alex's hips as he began to fuck her ass harder. It felt like their cocks were almost touching within her, just a thin layer of skin separating them. Sliding in and out of her and alternating back and forth.

Jacob's breathing changed, and then a moment later, so did Alex's.

And she was still building, like a volcano. All of the other orgasms that came before had been warnings. This was the big one.

She felt like she was going to erupt.

'Yes,' she said. 'Please, keep going. Harder.'

At her word both men let loose, pounding into her as she screamed their names, over and over.

'Yes. I'm going to cum,' she yelled into the night sky.

And she did.

Her whole body convulsed and twisted, she lost all control of her limbs, her eyes widened as her fingers splayed out and her hands and arms searched wildly for her men as they held her tight between them, feeling small and secure and safe.

Then she felt Jacob start to cum, pumping into her pussy, filling her with his seed and she came again. It was like a rolling orgasm, each wave stronger than the last.

Now she felt Alex throbbing, and the inside of her ass felt warm as he exploded into her and she was over the precipice and off the edge.

For a moment, it seemed like she blacked out.

There was nothing but energy and ecstasy, and her and them.

Bliss.

Perfection.

As her senses returned she regained control of her tingling body and she felt her two men softening inside her, their bodies spent and rippling and sweating against hers.

She didn't want them to pull out, she wanted them to stay inside her for as long as they could. As long as they were inside her, they were one. The feeling of wholeness was everything she had ever wanted. She never wanted it to end.

Being careful not to move too much, she looped her arms around the necks of both men and pulled them closer to her. In turn they wrapped their arms across her stomach and breasts, then their legs across hers like a cocoon, and together they cuddled and kissed.

Neither man pulled away, both pressed against her as tight as they could.

Their seed inside her.

Loving her as she loved them.

It had been everything she had ever wanted.

The perfect ending, to the perfect day.

As Rose slowly drifted off to sleep, she whispered.

'I love you both. I love you, both.'

*

Rose woke up smiling.

The sun was shining warmly on her face, soothing her awake with its gentle touch and as she opened her eyes she saw the most magnificent view.

A full inversion.

She sat up.

Below her, starting just a hundred or so feet beneath the edge of the cliff upon the top of which they had camped, was a thick layer of cloud which stretched off into the horizon, punctured here and there by magnificent mountains piercing through the clouds like islands in a churning sea of white.

Rose had never seen anything like it.

It was as though she had floated up to heaven during the night and was now looking out upon a whole new world of wonder and beauty.

At some point during the evening, one of the two men had woken and lain their sleeping bags across them all, topped with a thick blanket that was most likely Jacob's. She felt cosy, breathless and completely and utterly at peace.

Jacob was beginning to stir beside her and as he woke up he squeezed her, looking up at her face as she gazed out over the landscape, the sun still rising.

As he turned to look, she heard him draw breath and sit up, the blanket falling away from them both.

'Oh wow,' he said, in a whispered awe.

Alex rolled over and opened his eyes, rubbing them and then looked at the pair of them staring into the distance. He frowned and turned.

'Oh shit, would you look at that?'

For a while they all watched as the sun rose, the light illuminating the clouds in a golden radiant hue.

Rose reached out and took Alex and Jacob's hands in her own, pulling them closer to her and squeezing them softly.

'I want this,' she said. 'This is what I've always wanted.'

'Can this work though?' said Jacob.

'If we want it to, it can,' said Rose.

'Do we want it to?' said Alex.

Rose didn't say anything, she didn't need to answer. They knew what she wanted.

'I'm willing to give it a go,' said Jacob.

They both turned to look at Alex, who looked away, hand on his chin, elbow resting on his knee.

Rose held her breath, waiting for him to respond.

'I think I might need a little more persuasion,' said Alex, turning back and winking.

Rose smiled broadly, she reached under the blanket with her hand and searched between his legs and then her eyes widened.

'Oh, good morning,' she said, laughing. 'I don't think you're going to need much convincing at all.'

Alex pounced on her and she screamed in delight as he kissed her neck and caressed her breasts. Jacob grinned as he watched the pair of them, listening to Rose squeal as Alex ran his hands across her stomach and hips.

As Alex kissed her chest, Rose reached out for Jacob and pulled him close to her face and kissed him and then she pressed her forehead against his and looked deep into his eyes.

'I want you both,' she said. 'I love you both. Be with me, please.'

'We always have been, Rose,' said Jacob and he kissed her back.

*

EPILOGUE

One Year Later

Jacob pushed open the door to the hotel room and stepped inside. The lights were off, but the glow that shone in through the windows illuminated the space in a swathe of neon pinks, purples and greens.

The room was high up in the city, and the view was humbling, the door slowly swung closed as he walked across to the window and looked out and down at the streets hundreds of meters below.

In the distance Tokyo tower shone like a beacon of light, its glow emanating out across the clouds which lay low above the city, beginning to gather and spread out beneath them.

His focus shifted and he watched in the reflection of the window as Alex walked into the room behind him.

'Didn't want to turn the lights on then?' he said, dropping this bag down next to Jacob's.

'Didn't want to ruin the view.'

'Oh wow,' said Alex, walking over to stand next to his friend. 'Reminds me of the Alps.'

Jacob nodded.

'I miss her,' he said.

'Me too,' said Alex.

They both stood staring out of the window for a moment, thinking back.

'I've only been gone a week,' said Rose.

Both men jumped and turned.

'What the fuck?' said Alex. 'Rose?'

Jacob looked toward the middle of the room as his eyes adjusted to the darkness.

There, laying on the bed was Rose, but it was too dark to make her out properly.

'When did you get here?' said Alex.

'About four hours ago,' she laughed. 'Got a flight over from the Gotjawal Forest in South Korea. I've spent a lot of time soaking wet, trudging through wetland and reading some *very* smutty books.'

Alex was moving towards the light switch, but Rose stopped him.

'Wait,' she said.

He watched as her supple silhouette leaned across the silk bed sheets and clicked on the small side light attached to the wall beside the huge queen sized bed.

'Oh, shit,' said Alex.

Jacob's eyes widened.

Rose was dressed in a red lace chemise, and thigh high stockings with suspenders that clipped onto a pair of small lacy knickers. As the two men watched, Rose parted her legs to reveal that they were crotchless.

Alex bit his knuckle and exhaled. Jacob just stared, his mouth wide open.

'Welcome to Tokyo, boys,' said Rose, smiling. 'I hope you've enjoyed your travels. I was hoping I might be your reward.'

Alex and Jacob smiled as they walked towards her, kneeling onto the bed one after the other.

As they did, Rose saw that same look that always thrilled her and filled her with a mixture of fear and intense arousal.

Her two lions were back and she was in their lair.

Their helpless prey.

And she couldn't have been happier.

THE END

I hope you enjoyed the story of Rose, Jacob and Alex. If you did, then don't worry, this won't be the end of their adventures.

THANK YOU

Thank you for reading **Sharing Rose**, I really hope you've enjoyed it as much as I *loved* writing it. If you did, would you please spare a few moments to rate it, or even write a short review on Amazon? Even just a couple of lines makes a HUGE difference. I would be so grateful! It really helps other amazing readers like yourself feel confident in giving a new author a try.

If you have the time to rate it, or leave a review on Goodreads or BookBub too, that would be incredible! x

OTHER BOOKS

Be With Us

It started as a forbidden fantasy. A wife's desire to make love with another couple. But making new friends is complicated. A loving spouse, his faithful wife; the girl of her dreams, and her alpha husband. Will opening up their perfect marriage be a step too far? Or will it be a journey of sexual awakening that will transform their lives forever...

An urban foursome love story about Emilia and Cassian, a loving and faithful husband and wife, who take their fantasy out of the bedroom, and unexpectedly discover a much deeper and more powerful connection with another couple than they ever anticipated.

During the first two weeks of release, **Be With Us** became a **#1 Bestseller** on **Amazon**.

* * *

Buy it now on Kindle or read it for free on Kindle Unlimited

*

Follow me on Amazon to be notified when my next book is out!

ABOUT THE AUTHOR

BRIANNA SKYLARK is the pen name of a happily married, utterly insatiable, thirty-something mother of two living in a repressed little village on the south coast of England.

She's the wife of a rugged archeologist and often likes to think she's married to Indiana Jones. Over the years she's experimented with various occupations including filmmaking, video game voiceover artist and climbing instructor, but her favourite job is her most recent one... steamy romance novelist.

She loves bringing sweet, strong, faithful and loving women to life through her books, and then introducing them to strong, kind and endearing alpha males (or sensual females) who satisfy their every desire in the bedroom and beyond.

When she's not writing, she's often found hiking or climbing in the far reaches of Scotland and Wales or exploring the woods and beaches near her home with the man of her dreams, and their two gorgeous children.

Follow me on Amazon, Twitter, Goodreads & BookBub

www.briannaskylark.com
Short, secret, sexy and sweet.

Printed in Dunstable, United Kingdom